The Stars of Locust Ridge

CRAIG MOODY

Visit us at: www.vividimagerypublishing.com

Vivid Imagery Publishing
www.vividimagerypublishing.com

Vivid Imagery Publishing print and digital first edition November 2018

Vivid Imagery Publishing books may be purchased in bulk for educational, business, fund-raising, or sales promotional use. For information, please e-mail Promotions@vividimagerypublishing.com.

Publishers Note: This book is a work of fiction. Any references to historical events, real people, or real places are used fictitiously. Other names, characters, places, and events are products of the author's imagination, and any resemblance to actual events or places or persons, living or dead, is entirely coincidental.

Cover art photography by Mark Andrew Thomas
Edited by Stacey Kopp

Printed in the United States of America

ISBN 978-0-9986558-9-5 (Hardcover)
ISBN 978-1-7328960-0-0 (Paperback)
ISBN 978-1-7328960-1-7 (Kindle)
ISBN 978-1-7328960-2-4 (eBook)
ISBN 978-1-7328960-3-1 (Audiobook)

THE STARS OF LOCUST RIDGE

Dedicated to my Pepa:
The first person to tell me about the moving stars.

I T WAS EARLY MARCH 1973 THE FIRST TIME I SAW THE STARS move over Locust Ridge, Tennessee. I had just turned sixteen the previous summer, my blossoming woman-hood suddenly apparent seemingly overnight. I had been born and raised in Locust Ridge, a tiny area of Appalachia, now on the map due to the budding career of our county's queen, Ms. Dolly Parton. Born in 1946, Dolly escaped the confines of severe poverty, which continues to plague these mountains, the day after she graduated from high school. Now a star on television's *The Porter Wagoner Show*, her most recent single, "My Tennessee Mountain Home," can currently be heard sweetening the sound of the nation's country music radio airwaves, melodizing Dolly's girlhood experience of the same hills and hollers that defined my own childhood.

Stumbling along the path that led from the small one-bed-room house I shared with my momma to the log cabin where her only brother, my uncle John, lived, my feet led the way by memory as my eyes stared into the heavens.

Like flittering hummingbirds, seven stars flickered and darted over the night sky in unison. Pausing in place, each would move again in formation, suddenly and rapidly, so quickly that they seemed to appear in their next position before your eyes could even capture the movement. I had never seen anything like it.

"Uncle John!" I called as I neared his cabin, a quaint structure straight out of an old-timey Smoky Mountain fairy tale. "Come quick! You haveta see this!"

I kept my eyes locked on the darting stars, their bright glow easily and obviously outshining any of the other stars behind them.

"What?" Uncle John mumbled, shuffling out onto his front porch.

"Look!" I shouted, pointing up to the sky without looking at him.

Then, as if aware of his presence, the stars froze, their wheeling and darting now still and static.

"What am I looking at, Gen?" Uncle John questioned, squinting his eyes to gain a clearer view of the moonless sky above us.

"Those stars," I answered, pointing out all seven individually. "They was just movin', I swear. Dartin' around like little bugs."

I could feel Uncle John's eyes on me even before I looked at him.

"Uncle John, I ain't makin' this up, I swear it. They was just flittin' around all fast. So fast that I could barely see 'em move. They would just be in the next spots as if they'd always been there."

Uncle John just stared at me blankly, the smell of his homemade moonshine dominating his breath.

"Gen," he started, clearing his throat before continuing. "Have you been messin' in that jar of peach brew I sent over to your momma yesterday?"

"Oh stop," I snapped, clearly annoyed at the ridiculous accusation.

I peered up toward the heavens, and my heart skipped a beat as I realized all seven stars had disappeared. Vanished. They were completely gone from the night sky as though they had never been there at all.

"Wha—?" my voice cracked.

Uncle John followed my gaze.

"Come on, Gen," he urged, returning to the cabin door.

"But, Uncle John, you haveta believe me; they was dartin' around and flickerin'—"

Uncle John's smile broke my thought.

"Just come on in," he motioned, pulling the door open. "I just put some stew on the stove."

Taking one last look at the stars, I shook my head at my own disbelief. Perhaps I was just seeing things. Momma was always scolding me for adding a bit too much imagination to nearly everything I said.

As old as Uncles John's cabin was, the smell of fresh pine still ruminated from the logs as though they had only been cut down and assembled just yesterday. The aroma was overwhelmed by the smell of Uncle John's beef stew the moment I passed the threshold. Closing the wooden cabin door behind me, I drifted toward the kitchen area of Uncle John's large one-room cabin and sat at the two-chair kitchen table. Every single piece of furniture in Uncle John's cabin had been handcrafted by him. Anything and everything that was made of wood had been chopped, sanded, nailed, and varnished. The only structure he had not created himself was the cast-iron stove and porcelain washing bin. Even the bed and couch frame had been hand-designed by him, although the mattress and sitting cushions had been stuffed and hand-sewn by my momma.

Uncle John and Momma were four years apart, raised in these same hills by their momma and daddy. I had never met any of my grandparents. Uncle John and Momma's parents died before I was born, and I never got to know my daddy at all, not to mention his kinfolk.

"I pulled these carrots just this mornin'," Uncle John announced from the stove. "They been comin' in so good this year."

I smiled and nodded, still confused and disturbed by what I had just witnessed outside. How was it possible that seven stars could move in unison and then suddenly disappear as if they had never even been there in the first place?

"When does your momma come home this week?" Uncle John asked, perhaps noticing my distance.

"Uh..." I began, forcing my thoughts from their random spin of obsession over the moving stars. "Wednesday, I think."

Momma was an assistant manager at a motel in Gatlinburg. Gatlinburg wasn't all that far away, but considering the distance, time, and cost to travel, Momma simply stayed at the motel during her consecutive work days, returning home only when she had at least a day or two off. There were times when I wouldn't see her for nearly two full weeks, sometimes three.

It was a blessing that Uncle John lived so close. A single man at age thirty-seven, he had only been married once. It ended when I was still in grade school, and there were no children to speak of. I often stayed the night with Uncle John. He would always take the couch, allowing me full reign of his worn and unevenly stuffed mattress. Most nights, though, I suppose as a subconscious effort not to allow loneliness and fear get the best of me, I opted to stay home alone. Despite being raised in these hills, the billowing night sounds that haunted the midnight hour could be overwhelming, if not downright terrifying, to any grown man, never mind an adolescent girl. Still, I knew Uncle John was only a short walk away, and that provided me the security and comfort I needed to operate and thrive in my circumstantial solitude.

"Alright," Uncle John exclaimed, pulling the large wooden stirring spoon from his scarred and dented copper cooking pot. "Let's eat!"

My mind continued to wander, while Uncle John sucked down his stew. Nervous and bit upset, I sporadically poked at my dish, pulling various morsels of beef and vegetables from the mix and placing them onto my tongue to avoid Uncle John's notice.

"How's school been this year?" Uncle John broke the silence, lifting his dark-brown eyes to my pale-blue ones. "You out of junior high now, right?"

"High school, yes," I agreed, keeping my focus on the bowl before me.

"How you likin' your new teachers and all? The kids treatin' ya right?"

I nodded in silence.

"What about that Emily girl? She still givin' ya any trouble?"

My stomach lurched at the sound of Emily's name. For as long as I could remember, Emily Watson, daughter of Jeffery and Pamela Watson, owners of nearby Sevierville's largest drugstore, bullied and harassed me simply for existing. Momma had to insist I be switched into another class back in fourth grade due to Emily's abuse. When she wasn't ragging on me for my hair or looks, she was pinching, poking, or prodding me with writing utensils, even going as far as putting dirt and glue into a jelly sandwich I had brought one day for lunch. How she managed to steal the paper-bag-sealed sandwich and lace it with the spiteful and unappetizing foreign contents was still a mystery to me to this day. Unfortunately, with Sevierville, the closest town to Locust Ridge, being so quaint and small, Emily was in three of my new four classes. Although the new semester had only just begun a month prior, I could already sense the brutality and hatred that was soon to be dished my way. I had already met eyes with Emily twice, and both times, her glare raged a fire and palpable venom that stole my breath and tripped the rhythm of my beating heart.

"Well, you let me know if she starts givin' ya trouble again," Uncle John continued, keeping his eyes fixed over mine. "I'll have a chat with her daddy if need be."

I remained silent, suddenly overwhelmed with the emotional whirlwind that the very thought of Emily Watson conjured. At least the distraction had eased my mind from its obsessive ruminating regarding the moving stars and back onto something earth-bound.

"Ya gonna stay over here tonight, or head back on over to your place?"

"I guess I best get back home," I said, dropping my spoon against the side of the bowl. "I have some homework to finish up."

Uncle John nodded, his pink lips smiling in the dim light of the nearby kerosene lamp.

I kept my eyes locked on the night sky as I ventured the familiar path through the thick woods that separated Uncle John's cabin from Momma's and my house. Now amongst the trees, I could no longer see the sky, only the complete blackness of the world around me.

Once home, I decided to go straight to bed. To my own surprise, I didn't stand out in the yard ceaselessly gawking at the sky. Instead, I entered the house, scribbled out the last bit of my remaining homework, and dropped my exhausted body onto my twin-sized bed, the same one I had slept in since age five. I was lucky to have my own room. Momma had switched our beds around about two years ago, placing her full-sized mattress in the corner of the living room, allowing me the comfort and privacy of my own dresser, full-length mirror, window, and door. In Locust Ridge, having your own bed, let alone your own room with a functioning door, was considered much more than a luxury.

I kicked off my shoes just as I began to drift. I could have sworn I saw a flash of lighting illuminate the window as my lids fell heavy and my brain gave way to unconsciousness. I would have taken a thunderstorm, a tornado even, compared to the personal chaos and hell that was to begin the very next morning.

***

I AWOKE TO THE sound of Uncle John reentering the cabin. Confused, I sat up, still tucked tight beneath the heavy quilt of his bed.

"Mornin', sunshine," I heard Uncle John say as he closed the cabin door behind him. "Outhouse is a bit raw at the moment, so I suggest you hold everything in for a bit if ya can."

I shook my head.

"Why am I here?" I questioned, peering around the room as though it were the first time I had ever seen it.

"Ya mean ya don't remember what happened?" Uncle John spoke as he carried out the task of preparing coffee on the stove.

"Remember what?"

"I found ya in the woods last night, around midnight... howlin' and a'screamin' like a wildcat."

He didn't turn around. Instead, he continued to focus on the simmering aluminum stovetop percolator.

My heart began to accelerate, my hearing narrowing into a hollow drone.

"I don't understand. The last thing I remember, I was in my bed. How on earth did I manage to make it out into the woods?"

Uncle John didn't answer, perhaps aware that I was speaking more to myself than to him.

"Well, whatever the case may be, you was out in the woods, screamin' in such a way as I have never heard another human being scream before. I haveta say, I was pretty damn worried."

My mind continued to spin; a feeling of cold isolation and terror of the unknown washed over and pricked at my skin.

"Here," Uncle John said calmly, a tin mug of fresh black coffee in his hand.

Taking the mug from his grasp, I racked my brain for an explanation. The feeling of not being able to account for such an event was far more overwhelming and disturbing than one who had never experienced such a thing would imagine. Not even the warmth of the black coffee could melt the chill that draped my entire body.

"Ya better get ready for school. I think it's best you just carry out your regular routine. This, whatcha had, was more than likely just what they call a night terror...or night walkin'. You'll be okay. The important thing is ya wasn't hurt or nothin'."

I just stared at Uncle John, still lost in the confusion of my brain.

"Come on."

I followed Uncle John without hesitation as he led me back home.

"Stop ya worryin', Gen." He smiled as he placed a hand over my shoulder. "You gonna be okay. Stranger things have most certainly happened to other folks. Ya just lucky I'm right here to look after ya."

I watched for a long moment as Uncle John returned to the woods that would lead him back to his cabin.

Slowly and methodically, I washed my face, brushed my teeth, and dressed for school. Donning my favorite pair of denim overalls, work boots, and my hair slipped carelessly in a ponytail, I grabbed an apple and headed out the door to where the school bus would soon be arriving.

I didn't speak to another soul during the half-hour-long bus ride into Sevierville. No one seemed to mind nor care about my silence.

Once inside my homeroom, I pulled my homework from my stained and tattered knapsack and spread it over my desk. It took my brain several seconds to register the thump to the side of my head. I looked up just in time to see Emily Watson passing me on her way to her seat at the back of the classroom.

I scribbled notes and perfected various doodles as Mrs. Rangold filled the classroom with the sound of her voice. I wasn't quite sure what she was even going on about. All I could think of was what Uncle John had told me. The prospect of being alone out in the woods at midnight was terrifying, to say the least, not to mention the fact that I couldn't even remember it.

I munched on my apple as I sat alone in the cafeteria. The sound of the capacity-filled space echoed and warbled around my ears, but I didn't really notice or home in on any one specific conversation. It was only when Emily Watson approached me that I broke from my trance.

"Ya look like shit today," she scolded, her usual sidekicks standing on either side of her. To her right was Beverly Bishop, a freshman now in her third repeat of the grade. To her left, Tabitha Paul, a gorgeous, blonde sophomore who had much more than the male student body at notice. More than once I had seen Coach Jefferies, the school's only physical education coach, unable to remove his eyes from Tabitha. Tabitha was quite aware of the attention she garnered, but she was far too immature and insecure to do anything about it. Instead, she remained nearly sealed to the side of her group leader, Emily, a girl far less beautiful and appealing. Emily seemed to know this, for she ensured a daily hammering of not-so-playful jabbing and insults toward Tabitha, just enough to keep a stronghold on the poor girl's already fragile self-worth.

"What's the matter?" Emily continued when I failed to provide her a response. "Did your momma forget to make it home this month to hose ya off?"

I looked down as the three girls laughed.

"I'm talkin' to ya!" Emily commanded, smacking my forehead with an open hand.

Without a word or so much as a sound, I lifted from my seat and made my way to the nearest trash can. Disposing of my only half-consumed apple, I exited the cafeteria and headed toward my next class.

The bus ride home was no different than the one to school. I sat in silence, my eyes and mind lost to the flashing images of an imagined scene in the woods. Visualizing myself screaming and bellowing amongst the trees was all I could think of. How long was I out there before Uncle John found me? Was it possible that this had happened before but I'd somehow made it back inside and into bed, therefore unaware of the episode? The icy grip of fear of the unknown only tightened as I journeyed my way back home. I didn't hear Uncle John call my name as I entered the house.

"Hey," he said breathlessly as he entered the front door. "Didn't ya hear me callin' ya? I said your name at least ten times as you walked up the road past my place."

I just shook my head, unable and uninterested in speaking.

"How was school?"

I winced, the memory of the encounter with Emily still raw and fresh.

"What happened?" Uncle John questioned, stepping closer to me.

"Nothin', Uncle John. I don't wanna talk about school. I just wanna lie down for a while."

Uncle John only watched as I gulped down a glass of room-temperature water and shuffled to the couch. He never said another word as I drifted off to sleep.

***

THE HOUSE WAS DARK when I finally awoke some several hours later. On the kitchen table: a foil-wrapped meal. Uncle John had left a plate full of mashed potatoes, gravy, and what I assumed was pork, perhaps venison. Uncle John only ate what he grew and killed, so whatever it was, I could be sure it was clean and fresh.

I ate in silence, only the relentless hiss of the kerosene lamp making a sound.

I was just about to head to bed, when I heard footsteps on the front porch. Assuming it was Uncle John again, I was surprised to see my mother, still dressed in her work uniform, appear through the front door.

"Hey, hon," she exclaimed, an obvious strain of stress and exhaustion gripping her expression. "How are ya, babe?"

I smiled and nodded as she lowered her various bags, purse, and car keys. I closed my eyes as she secured her lips to my forehead, keeping them there just long enough to warm the ceaseless chill that had overtaken my body since I had awoken this morning.

"Ya doin' okay? Ya look tired."

"I'm fine, Momma. How's the motel?"

"Ugh," she sighed. "It's killin' me is what it's doin'. Mr. Barnes took a week off to take his wife and kids out to Nashville, so I'm runnin' double duty just tryin' to keep up. I swear, Gatlinburg is becomin' more and more touristy as each day goes by. Good for business, but hell on my nerves."

I watched in silence as she pulled several packs of cigarettes from her purse.

"Don't bother scoldin' me, hon," she whispered, pulling one of the solid-white cylinders from its carton, lighting it, and taking a long, drawn-out drag. "I know ya hate that I do this, and I've tried to quit, ya know that, but with all that's been goin' on at work recently, I just need somethin' to help take the edge off."

She peered around the room, resting her eyes on one of Uncle John's jars of moonshine.

"Hey, I suppose it's a hell of a lot better than suckin' down some of my brother's shine all day," she laughed, more to herself than to me.

"Ya been eatin'?" she asked, eyeing me up and down sus-piciously. "Ya look too thin, hon."

"Yeah," I mumbled. "I ain't been all that hungry lately, but Uncle John's been makin' sure I eat."

"Good." She smiled, relishing another long, silent drag of her cigarette.

My mother and I enjoyed an hour of television together, the two us side by side on the couch, laughing as one at *The Sonny and Cher Comedy Hour*. She kissed me goodnight before heading to her still-unmade bed in the corner of the room. I gazed lovingly and longingly at her for several seconds before turning in the direction of my bedroom.

I missed my mother, something I never told her. As much as I loved, needed, and admired my Uncle John, there was still nothing like a young girl's bond with her mother. I drifted to sleep with the smell of my momma's skin still on my mind. The scent of her subtle perfume was a substance I could trace back to the faded yet still potent memories of my early childhood. My last thought before unconsciousness was of Emily Watson, her broad forehead and wide nose twisted and pinched into a scowl, her two sycophant cling-ons cack-ling at her side. I hated Emily Watson, and one day, perhaps soon, I was going to do something about it.

***

MOMMA WAS ALREADY AWAKE when my alarm bell rang the next morning. Sitting at the kitchen table with a cigarette and coffee, she smiled as I entered the room, but her mouth quickly twisted into a frown as I neared her.

"Aren't those the same overalls ya had on yesterday?" she asked, eyeballing me from head to toe.

"Yes," I murmured, uncaring as to the fact that I had been wearing the same outfit pretty much the entire school week.

"We need to take ya into town for some shoppin'," Momma replied, tapping cigarette ash into a nearby glass ashtray. "Ya gettin' older now, Genevieve. We need to present ya as a bit more womanly."

I shrugged at the suggestion. I honestly did not care what I wore to school. My overalls were practical and comfortable, and I felt at peace and secure in them. I felt no need to change what had been working for me for years.

"What about your cycle?" Momma continued, twisting her cigarette in her fingers. "Ya started that yet?"

"Yes. Three years ago," I confirmed in an annoyed mumble.

"Good." Momma winked, nodding her head toward the bathroom. "Ya know I keep feminine hygiene products under the sink. They're for you to use. I have my own back at the motel."

"I know, Momma. Thank you."

"Now, come and get ya some breakfast. I don't want ya late for school."

I kissed Momma goodbye and made my way down the pathway from the house that led to the road. I saw Uncle John at the edge of his property, shirtless and glistening with per-spiration. My heart skipped a beat at the sensational display of manliness, but my brain quickly scolded me for perceiving my own flesh and blood in a lustful manner.

I didn't disturb him, nor did he see me as I passed his dirt driveway and rounded the corner to the crossroad where the bus stop was.

I thought of Momma and her sacrifice of giving up so much time with me, her one and only child and daughter, just to keep food on the table. I never knew who my daddy was, and Momma never said too much about him. What she did say wasn't very positive and most certainly suggested that I dare not pester her on the issue any further. All I knew was that he ran out on Momma not long after I was born, the tragic reality of so many women throughout human history.

I was nearly to homeroom, when Emily stepped into my path.

"Still look like shit," she smirked, only one of her minions, Beverly, by her side. "You are so disgustin'."

With that, she flipped her hair and sashayed away.

God, how I despised her. One of these days, I swear it, I was just going to knock her over and rightfully pummel her in that plain, smug mug of hers. The scary thought was, I knew that when it eventually happened, I was more than likely going to be out of control and unable to limit or contain myself.

I was just about to head to third period, when I saw him: Kenneth Reynolds, the one and only boy I had ever fancied. He caught my gaze and smiled. To my horror, he began to make his way in my direction.

"Hey, Genevieve," he spoke softly, stepping close enough that I could smell his faint cologne.

"Hey, Kenneth." I blushed, my face ablaze with awkward embarrassment.

"How ya been?" he continued, leaning his right arm against the nearest locker.

"Good," I muttered, clutching my old and worn knapsack tightly between my arms.

"Nice weather we been havin' lately, huh?"

I nodded, keeping my eyes focused on the floor.

"I'd like to come by sometime. Maybe take ya into town."

I looked up, utterly shocked by the suggestion.

"Me?" I managed to ask. "But I thought you was with Tabitha Paul?"

"Nah," he shook his head. "That ended around Christmas."

"Oh," I replied, the burning of my cheeks more inflamed than before.

"Well, how 'bout Saturday?" Kenneth suggested, pulling his arm from the locker and standing straight. "I'd love to take ya down to Watsons for a soda."

Without thought or any form of self-control, I agreed, resulting in a peck on the cheek and a confirmation of a date and time.

I walked on air for the rest of the school day, even finding myself skipping a bit as I rounded the corner of the old road that led me home.

Uncle John was still out in his yard. This time, he saw me and called out my name.

"You look happy," he observed as he neared me.

"I had a nice day at school," I replied, almost in song.

"That's good to hear," he nodded, smiling as he wiped his brow with an old red handkerchief.

I couldn't help but admire his naked torso as he returned the rag to his right-side jeans pocket.

"What made today better than the rest of the week? I could tell you've been down most of the time."

"Well..." I sputtered, my disbelief and nervousness regarding Kenneth Reynolds still too fresh and uncontrollable to risk mentioning. "I don't know. It was just good. No reason, I suppose."

Still panting from the stress of his manual labor, Uncle John nodded over his shoulder toward my house.

"Your momma still here?" he asked.

"I'm not sure. She came in last night, but she didn't say when she was headin' back to Gatlinburg."

"Well, if she's still around, tell her I've fixed supper for the both of ya. It'll be nice for us all to sit down as a family for once."

Smiling, I agreed, and continued my bounding gait toward the house.

Thankfully, Momma was still at home, busy ironing a stack of her work uniforms.

"Hey, hon." She smiled, a freshly lit cigarette dangling in the corner of her mouth. "How was your day?"

I couldn't help it. I was still far too amped and excited not to tell someone. For whatever reason, I felt far more at ease and comfortable detailing my encounter with Kenneth with my mother than I felt I could have been with Uncle John. Perhaps it was a female thing.

Momma just smiled and listened as I relived for her every single word and moment shared with Kenneth. She waited until I was done before stubbing out her still-unfinished cigarette.

"Gen, hon, I think it's time we talk."

I was nervous as I followed her to the kitchen table.

"Now, I don't know what ya know about what goes on between a man and a woman and whatnot, but I wanna be sure ya got a good head on ya before anything happens that you will regret."

I squirmed in my seat. I dreaded this conversation, but I knew it had to be had. In fact, it was needed. All I knew about sex was what I had seen and read in the stash of dirty magazines Uncle John kept hidden under his mattress. I had found them there a year or so ago when I was helping him tidy up. My heart raced as I viewed the unabashed display of human genitalia, women groping themselves, and men with engorged penises. I had revisited them once when I knew Uncle John was not at home. It was the first time I had ever masturbated, and I still thought of the raunchy pictures to this day. Still, I knew much of what I was seeing was posed and fantasy. I was still curious and hopeful that my mother would help to fill in some of the gaps.

"Now, see, boys your age, well, they just startin' to get the urges," she started, pulling a fresh cigarette from a nearby carton. "You sixteen now, so ya might even have some urges of your own."

I blushed and lowered my head.

"There ain't nothin' wrong with that, honey; it's just natural. But even still, ya now old enough to get ya'self in a whole world'a trouble if ya ain't careful. Don't move too fast with a boy just 'cause he wants somethin' from ya. A good boy will be patient and will work to earn it."

She lowered her eyes to her cigarette, inhaling a mouthful of smoke before removing the paper cylinder from her lips. "And a good girl won't just give it to him either. A good girl will know when the time is right. Timin' is everything in this life."

I kept my head down, my eyes counting the stains on my work boots.

"Now, I ain't delusional neither," Momma continued, lifting my chin with her finger. "I ain't gonna spit out preacher talk and suggest ya wait till ya married. Not a single soul I know has ever done that. Well, perhaps my mammie and pappy, but that was a different world back in their day. It's the seventies now. The modern world. Hell, I hear of girls at age twelve startin' on the pill. I just find that a bit ridiculous, so all I'm sayin' to my own daughter is, wait. Be patient, but most of all, honey, be damn careful."

I nodded, my chin still resting on her finger.

"Now, we gonna take ya into town tomorrow as soon as ya get in from school. I can't have my only daughter headin' out on her very first date in a pair of raggedy-ass overalls she's had since the fourth grade."

We laughed together, and for just a moment, I wished that my momma never had to leave for work again.

Later that evening, Momma and I walked hand in hand over to Uncle John's cabin. Displayed like a Christmas Day feast over his two-seat kitchen table was a platter of freshly baked ham, turnips, cabbage, baked potatoes, and what appeared to be a pecan pie. The smell was wonderful, and my heart was overfilled with present comfort and joy. It wasn't often that my mother and uncle stood in the same room. Despite my mother's need of her brother as both child supervisor and various household chore handyman, theirs was a complicated and secretive past. I wasn't quite sure of the details, but from actions more so than words, I knew something had occurred between them that had forever tainted their sibling relationship.

Tonight, though, none of that mattered. Momma laughed at Uncle John's jokes, and I savored and absorbed every single second of this momentary bliss.

With each dish depleted and the pecan pie annihilated, Uncle John shooed us from the kitchen when Momma and I attempted to start the dishes. As he escorted us home, I walked behind him and my mother, listening as they recounted a shared memory of life with their parents, a time and people I myself would never know.

I went to sleep that night in peace, dancing thoughts of family contentment and unprecedented romantic daydreaming leading me into my night dreams.

***

"WAKE UP, BABY," I heard my Momma coo, almost as if she were waking an infant. "I haveta go."

In the corner of my eye, I could see my bedroom window; the sun had only just begun to peek out above the nearest tallest treetops.

"I should be home in a week," she continued, pulling my quilt back, exposing my skin to the damp morning air. "When Mr. Barnes returns, I'm gonna request some time off."

"But I thought you was gonna take me shoppin' when I got home from school today?" I asked, wiping my eyes, clearing them of the fading memory of unconscious dreaming.

"I know, honey, and I feel terrible that I can't, but the motel called about twenty minutes ago, so I haveta go."

She smiled at me, sadness in her eyes as she took in the sight of my obvious disappointment.

"I left forty dollars on the kitchen table for ya, extra on top of the grocery money. It's for ya dress. Pick out somethin' nice."

She leaned to kiss my forehead, but I moved from her reach, kicking my legs over the side of the bed and stomping off to the bathroom.

I waited until I heard her leave before exiting the tiny place which enclosed the cracked porcelain bathtub, pull-chain toilet, and lopsided particleboard-encased fiberglass sink. I stared at myself in the mirror for a moment before pulling open the squeaking bathroom door. Staring back at me was the face of a little girl lost, once more abandoned and left to self-reliance by her one-remaining parental figure.

Uncle John was nowhere to be seen as I passed his property and traveled the short distance to the bus stop.

Discouraged and disappointed, I kept to myself the entire day, miraculously avoiding both Emily Watson and Kenneth Reynolds. I just knew I didn't have the courage to speak to Kenneth nor the tolerance to deal with Emily, so it was for the absolute best of all concerned that fate did not present any awkward encounters or forced interactions.

I decided on the bus ride home that I was still going to go forward with the date. Why should I allow the absence of Momma, both in general and for the shopping trip, to somehow dampen or discourage my living? I spent the majority of my time without her anyhow. Why was this to be any different? Still, in my heart, I knew my longing for her was heightened at the simple fact that I was venturing toward womanhood, and a young woman naturally wants and needs her mother to show her the way.

I caught sight of Uncle John's bare bottom as he stood urinating near a tree at the edge of the property line. Again, a surge of curiosity and excitement billowed through my veins. Once more disgusted at the very notion, I shook my head and focused my eyes on the dirt roadway. Thankfully, he didn't see me pass, so I was able to make it home uninterrupted.

Splashing cold water over my face, I retied my ponytail, changed into a fresh, clean T-shirt, pulled on one of my two decent denim jeans, and refastened my work boots.

I bounded off the front porch and entered the woods on the north side of the house. This path would take me to the train tracks, which, heading east, would lead me straight into the heart of Sevierville.

Of course, this route would take nearly four hours by foot. The more direct edge-of-town location of school could be reached far faster by vehicle, but I opted not to involve anyone on this journey. Asking Uncle John for a ride into town meant having to divulge the details of my planned date with

Kenneth, and asking one of the scattered hillside neighbors meant having to endure thirty-minute-long questions about school, my mother, life in general, and various other frivolous topics of discussion that I would rather not contend with.

I approached the tracks, and a strange ringing began to buzz behind my left ear. It was different than the usual ringing one experiences from time to time; this was far more concentrated, piercing, and palpable. I could actually feel the tender skin behind the cartilage of my left ear vibrating.

I stepped onto the center of the tracks, atop the old wooden planks that fell in succession, secured and fastened by the steel rails that ran parallel to each other.

Stepping back and forth between the steel and wood, I was amazed at how the ringing immediately ceased once on the wood but reignited with fury each and every time I neared or stepped directly on the rails. I kept amusing myself with the phenomenon throughout the several-mile-long journey into town.

Finally arriving in Sevierville, I left the tracks at Main Street, passing the hodgepodge of family-owned businesses, until I entered Bellman's, the inherited dress shop of Sevierville's mayor's wife, Virginia Morrison. Bellman was Virginia's maiden name, and the shop had been in her family for nearly a century, founded and established by her great-grandmother and passed down through the generations. Now the wife of the mayor, Virginia relegated the daily tasks and responsibilities to her younger sister, Susan, a loud-mouthed, vivacious, fireball of a woman who polarized those who encountered her. Most found her funny and amusing, but some of the townsfolk, especially the older women, found her to be vulgar and obnoxious but still dealt with her with polite Southern hospitality, mostly because they had no other choice but to shop at Bellman's. It was either that or venture the distance to nearby Knoxville. Most would rather just put up with Susan's relentless chatter and boastful bragging than deal with the drive, bus, or train ride to Knoxville.

Susan spotted me the very second the bell chime on the front door of the dress shop sounded throughout the building.

"Well, hey there, hon," she beamed, her caked-on makeup bright and overstated, even in the distance between us. "I don't think I've ever seen you in here before!"

I could smell her lilac perfume as she neared me, her navy-blue and white polka-dot dress and accompanying pearls tailored to fit to her body and neck as perfectly as a freshly plowed field.

"You're Eva Delany's girl, aren't ya?"

I nodded my head, cracking a nervous smile.

"Well, what can I do ya for, hon?"

My eyes trailed over the endless racks of colorful dresses, each one blending into the next. I only owned one dress, a solemn black velvet number Momma had given me to wear to church, a place we only went for the rare funeral or wedding. With Momma always in Gatlinburg and Uncle John practically a recluse, we didn't interact all that much with the neighbors in Locust Ridge, even less the townsfolk of Sevierville.

"I need a dress," I meekly stated, the sound of my voice as pinched and tight as Susan's bursting bosom.

"Well, you are certainly in the right place, sugar!"

I followed behind Susan as she led the way through the store, pulling various pieces from the racks, holding them over my chest, assessing and deciding upon their appearance. I let her do her thing, too unconcerned and nervous to really have much influence or input.

"What's the occasion, doll?" she asked after rejecting several brightly colored cotton one-pieces.

"Uh," I mumbled. "A date, I guess."

I felt my face fall crimson red as Susan burst into a fit of excitement.

"Oh, that's just wonderful, darlin!" she exclaimed, far more enthusiastically than what was called for. "And who is the lucky young man?"

I swallowed as I managed to mutter Kenneth's name.

The moment the name slipped from my lips, Susan's expression and demeanor changed.

"Ya mean Kenneth Reynolds, Tabitha Paul's beau?" she queried, her eyes narrowing.

"Well," I started, panic and fear accelerating my pulse and altering the colors of my skin.

"Never mind," Susan quickly continued, resuming her buoyant and oppressively joyful persona. "The goings-on of you youngin's ain't for my concern."

Nervously, I allowed Susan to shove several options at me for me to try on. One by one, I draped each garment over my body and exited the small dressing-room curtain for an embarrassing showcase for Susan. By the time I had on the third option, another customer had entered the store and now stood by Susan's side, nodding and accessing the outfit along with her. I cringed with humiliation as both women poked and prodded at my sides, adjusting the fit and squeezing my breasts. After nearly twenty minutes of fussing, pinning, altering, and turning, both women appeared satisfied. Susan eventually instructed me to remove the chosen garment, a solid-red cotton summer dress, so she could make what she felt were the necessary alterations.

"I can have it ready for ya by tomorrow afternoon," Susan explained once I returned to the counter after redressing into my simple white T-shirt and blue jeans.

She must have recognized the look of slight panic that resonated over my face.

"Is your date tomorrow, sweetie?" she cooed in a singsong voice, her expression now furrowed and frowned into a powder-thick mesh of loose skin.

I nodded.

"Well then—" she smiled "—I will personally deliver it and help ya get ready. How about that?"

I nodded again, smiling, unsure if it were a good idea or not.

The dress cost the full forty dollars, with Susan loudly announcing that she would drop the sales tax and alteration fee.

I thanked her, took my receipt, and managed my way from the store, which was now filled with several gawking women, both young and old, all curiously staring in my direction. I could hear them mumbling and whispering as I pulled open the shop door and returned to the sidewalk.

I was nearly back to the tracks, when I heard a familiar voice shout my name.

I peered over my shoulder to see Emily, moving in a semi-jog toward me. I pretended not to hear her and continued to the train track, ignoring the blatant ringing behind my left ear as I stepped over the rail.

"Hey!" she screamed, tugging at my shoulder.

Silently, I turned around.

"I just heard you is goin' out with Kenneth?" she exclaimed, breathless from her running.

I only stared.

"Is that true?" she questioned, closing the slight space between us into a mere inch or so. "Ya know that's Tabitha's man?"

"He told me they broke up around Christmas," I flatly replied, noticing the quickening of my pulse.

"Well, not exactly," Emily continued, the sting of her breath across my face hot and piercing. "As far as Tabitha's concerned, they just on a break. Not broken up."

I didn't speak further; instead, I allowed my eyes to shift over Emily's face, noting her very plucked eyebrows, powder-heavy complexion, and dramatic swaths of blush and eyeshadow. It must be so imprisoning and sad to live your life so locked and concerned over your image, working desperately to appear as someone you aren't. Emily was certainly no Bridgett Bardot, but she mimicked her makeup and hairstyle to a T.

"Ya better just stay away from him, Genevieve," she commanded, her tone aggressive but less confrontational than it was whenever she had her two sidekicks by her side. "If Tabitha finds out about this, she's gonna kick your ass."

I smirked, turned around, and began stepping over the wooden planks of the track, heading back in the direction of home.

"Hey!" Emily screamed, her voice echoing off the nearby trees. "Don't ya turn your back on me!"

Emily grabbed a fistful of my hair, and my head jerked backward as she yanked me toward her. Without thought or so much as a moment of hesitation, I spun around, clocking the side of her powder-thick face with my fist.

I stood silently as Emily fell to the ground, her knee scraping against one of the wooden planks of the track.

"You ugly bitch!" she screamed, attracting a few onlookers. "I fuckin' hate you!"

Turning around again, I said not a word as I moved into the distance of the nearby woods, Sevierville slowly vanishing from behind me.

I could hear Emily talking loudly to someone as I slowly faded from view. I felt both rattled and satisfied at the unexpected encounter. Hopefully, this would discourage further insults, threats, and intimidations at school. But, boy, I could not have been more wrong.

***

KENNETH WAS DUE AT my house at seven. Susan Bellman arrived promptly at six.

"Now, does your momma have any curlers?" Susan asked as she finished painting my face. "I wanna pile your hair up. I think it'll look just gorgeous curled at the edges."

I directed Susan to the under-sink cabinet in the bathroom, a space filled to the brim with Momma's paints, powders, potions, and various other beauty supplies that I never looked at nor bothered to mess with.

"Oh, perfect!" I heard Susan exclaim, reappearing in the kitchen with Momma's lime-green curling iron.

I zoned in and out as Susan filled the air with relentless chatter that was both a bit comforting and welcome. I was nervous enough as it was, so savoring Susan's distraction of mindless jabbering was somehow satisfying.

Fully dressed, bejeweled, and perfumed, I stood before the full-sized mirror in disbelief. I could not believe what I was seeing. The summer dress flowed flawlessly over my body, pulled tight in all the right places, extenuating the blossoming curves of my still-blooming womanhood. The small pearls, a gift from Susan, hugged my neck beautifully, and my hair and makeup were as perfect as any of the models' in the Sears catalog.

Susan paraded around the kitchen, fawning and clapping as excited as if I were her own daughter. A part of me was sad it wasn't Momma in her place, yet I was tremendously grateful to Susan for all that she had done.

"Thank you, Ms. Bellman." I smiled, my face still frozen toward the mirror. "I can't believe what I look like."

"Oh, honey," she exclaimed breathlessly, "you are more than gorgeous. And please, call me Susan, hon. Ms. Bellman is my momma's name."

I nodded at her in the mirror, still in complete disbelief at the grown woman staring back at me.

For the absolute first time in my entire sixteen years of existence, I felt beautiful. Not pretty, but absolutely beautiful.

Susan left just fifteen minutes before Kenneth arrived, handsome and dapper in his pressed slacks and dress shirt, his hair parted and combed like a movie star's.

"Wow," he whispered, more to himself than to me. "Ya look amazin', Genevieve."

Blushing, I thanked him.

I followed him to the car, a bright-green 1967 Lincoln Continental which belonged to his daddy.

Kenneth Reynolds was the son of the town's only doctor. Years ago, his momma had worked as his daddy's head nurse, but she now enjoyed the luxury of being a successful doctor's socialite and homemaker wife. Dr. Reynolds delivered most of the babies in Sevierville and in the various valleys and hollers like Locust Ridge. Needless to say, they were a well-off family, at least by Sevierville standards.

I saw Uncle John standing frozen and staring from the field behind his cabin as Kenneth and I drove down the dirt roadway toward the corner crossroad that would lead us to town.

I knew I was in for a world of questioning once I returned home.

"So," Kenneth broke the silence, lowering the volume of the car radio. "I hear ya knocked ol' fathead Emily to the ground yesterday."

I winced, the memory of the unpleasant encounter once again reaccelerating my pulse and fraying my nerves.

"Don't worry," he reassured me as we rounded the edge of Locust Ridge, "I think it's great. I ain't ashamed to say it, but Emily Watson is a spoiled little sass-mouth that I've never cared for. She did nothin' but butt in and try to control my relationship with Tabitha. She's half, well, nearly all the reason why I broke up with Tabitha in the first place. I just couldn't stand how obsessed Tabitha was with Emily and how much control and credence she allowed her to have over our lives."

I listened quietly as Kenneth went on to detail various instances that proved his point about Emily. Basically, dating Tabitha Paul meant Emily Watson was completely involved, like it or not.

We pulled up to Watson's Drugstore, the only drugstore in town and Emily's family's business, and parked. My stomach lurched nervously at the prospect of encountering Emily once we entered the store. She often worked the soda counter on various afterschool evenings and certain weekends. The last thing I wanted or needed now was for her to see me with Kenneth.

Thankfully, she was nowhere to be seen as Kenneth escorted me to the soda counter. The two of us hopped atop the stationary turn stools that lined the bar.

Kenneth let me order my own soda, something I had only enjoyed once in my lifetime, a birthday treat with Momma when I had turned eight. I had only vague memories of the sweetness of the ice cream and vanilla extract, a memory that became instantly heightened the very second the current soda passed my lips and over the taste buds of my tongue. Instantly, I flashed back to that day with Momma, a far simpler era, when she didn't spend as much time in Gatlinburg and I had yet to grow to miss her so.

I listened to Kenneth as he casually detailed the goings-on of his football team, the various practical jokes and pranks he and the other boys played on their coaches, and the aspirations he had to go professional someday.

Kenneth was a year older than me, the current school year his last. My heart fluttered when he reached out to touch my cheek, gently sweeping away a rogue eyelash, which had most likely fallen there due to the foreign weight of Susan Bellman's heavily applied mascara.

Exiting Watson's, we headed back to Dr. Reynold's parked Lincoln, when the voice of Emily Watson broke the casual bubble of the atmosphere.

"I told ya, Tabitha," she seethed, her left eye bruised and blackened, a lasting reminder of our previous encounter. "The ugly whore is with your man."

My heart raced as my eyes shifted to Tabitha, her pretty, soft face gnarled and twisted in a painful scowl, her fists clenched at her sides. Beverly Bishop stood beside them, her face grinning in silent anticipation of what was to come.

"How could ya, Kenny?" Tabitha choked. "I thought we was just on a break?"

I stepped back, moved by instinct. I felt out of place next to Kenneth as he sternly retorted Tabitha's assumption.

"No, Tabby, I made it very clear to you that night. It's over. I'm done. I've had enough."

"So ya go with some trash slut from the sticks?" Emily shouted, keeping her eyes locked on mine.

"Shut up, Emily!" Kenneth reacted. "You're most of the reason why I broke up with Tabitha in the first place."

"Oh, don't go there, Reynolds," Emily scoffed, shaking her head, finally moving her eyes off me and back to Kenneth. "We all know you dropped Tabitha because she wouldn't put out. Not like this whore you're with now."

I inched toward her, my fists gripped and locked. I would have decked her again, but Kenneth stopped me with his arm.

"Just get in the car, Genevieve," he whispered. "I'll take care of this."

Hesitant yet obedient, I backed off toward the car, closing the heavy passenger-side door shut beside me.

I fidgeted with the pearls that draped elegantly against the skin of my neck as Kenneth continued to bicker with both Emily and Tabitha.

Finally, with Tabitha in tears and Emily moving to comfort her, Kenneth turned from the encounter and walked to the driver-side door of his daddy's Lincoln.

"Go on with that slut!" Emily screamed from the doorway of her parent's drug store. "I bet she sucks cock just like her momma!"

My hand gripped the door handle, a rage and anger I had never known before moving my body from the car seat.

"Stop," Kenneth commanded, placing his arm across my chest. "Just let her go. She ain't worth a reaction."

I could feel the bare skin of my upper chest brushing across Kenneth's forearm as I slowly managed to calm the unprecedented inferno that now accelerated through my veins. It was one thing for Emily Watson to batter and abuse me with her names, but it was quite another for her to involve my momma.

Ten minutes later and we were back in the mountains, the houses and buildings of Sevierville slowly fading behind us.

My anger gave way to nervousness as Kenneth pulled the car over at the edge of an old, abandoned farm, a known make-out spot for the high-schoolers.

Cutting the ignition, the sound of the nearby woods instantly became clear and audible.

"I'm so glad you agreed to come out with me tonight." Kenneth smiled, his handsome face strong and chiseled. Several of my dirty-magazine-induced fantasies had involved Kenneth. Replacing the heads and faces of the strange, aroused men with the familiar memory of Kenneth's smile and glowing brown eyes had led me to climax on far more than one occasion. Still, despite the fantasy, I was nervous as hell while sitting alone with him in the dark car, the brilliant display of the star-littered heavens brightly illuminated above us.

"I think I better get back home now, Kenneth," I managed to speak, my voice meek and muffled beneath the chirping crickets and singing katydids that surrounded us.

"Aw, ya ain't gonna let ol' Emily get the best of us, are ya?" he asked, leaning closer, the smell of his musk cologne overtaking my nose. Instantly, I felt the lower regions of my body grow hot and begin to perspire. Uncomfortable, I squirmed in my seat, forcing my body back against the solid car door.

Kenneth paused, allowing his eyes to dart over my face and upper chest before smiling and nodding.

"Alright then," he agreed. "I may be a lot of things, but anything less than a perfect gentleman is certainly not one of 'em. No ma'am, this boy's momma raised him up right."

He winked and smiled bigger. I couldn't help but blush and smile in return. I was both curious and horrified at the physical reaction my body had to him, especially the scent of his cologne whenever he moved close to me. I had never encountered a moment where my own body did as it pleased, sweat and blood flow accentuating the intimacy of my inner thighs as if the entire lower region of my body had a mind all of its own.

Kenneth continued to fill the silence with mindless chitchat as we drove the dark mountain roads back to Locust Ridge. I listened intently but was mostly just anxious to get back home, remove the makeup and dress, put away the pearls, and bathe. No offense to Kenneth, but I had seen enough action for the evening to satiate a thousand date nights. All I wanted to do was return to my safe place: my home and the surrounding woods.

Uncle John's cabin windows glowed with the warm light of his kerosene lamp as the growling engine of the Lincoln ascended the car up the gravel pathway toward my house.

"Please," Kenneth began after he had escorted me from the car and onto the front porch, "don't let this be the last time we go out like this. I wanna get to know ya better, Genevieve. You are such a mysterious girl."

I smiled in the dim light from the moon as he pressed his lips to my hand, bowed and nodded like an old Southern gentleman, and returned to the side of the massive car.

I waved and continued to smile as I watched him turn the giant vehicle around and slip into the blackness of the distance.

I was just about to open the front door, when I heard Uncle John's voice, the smell of a joint suddenly obvious.

"When was ya gonna tell me you are seein' that boy?" Uncle John queried, moving out from the darkness of the farther end of the porch. It was obvious he had been waiting there.

"This was our first date, Uncle John," I answered. "What's there to tell? It ain't like I'm marryin' the boy or somethin'."

Uncle John stepped closer, the orange ember from the end of his rolled and packed marijuana causing his face to glow in a devilish illumination. My heart skipped slightly in fear.

"I understand that, Gen," he spoke, blowing a lungful mass of smoke beside him. "Just, with me as your primary guardian around here and all, I like to know where you goin' and with who."

He took another drag of his joint, his face again colored with the orange light of the burning grass.

"That's all, baby niece," he continued, lifting his hand to touch my face. "I realize you is growin' up. Ya look beautiful, by the way. Ya remind me of your momma the night of her junior prom."

I closed my eyes and smiled. I had only ever seen one photo of my momma from her junior prom, a small black-and-white picture Momma kept, still framed and hidden in the back of her closet hope chest. The chest remained locked, the key with Momma in Gatlinburg, so I had only viewed the picture one time when she had left the chest open after fetching some winter blankets.

"Thank you, Uncle John," I whispered, pressing my face into his hand. "I love you. I'm gonna go wash all this off now."

I felt him watch me as I entered the house, the powerful aroma of the marijuana fading as soon as I closed the front door.

Undressing and unfastening my hair and pearls, I slipped into the cracked tub and allowed myself the escape of memory and imagination.

Replaying the evening's events in my mind, I carefully scrubbed a warm washcloth over my face, seeing the mixture of paints and powders slide across the rag and into the water.

I slipped beneath the cover of the bed and followed the excitement of my brain, both positive and nerve-wracking, into the silence of sleep.

***

I AWOKE TO THE sound of a muffled voice and an extreme pain radiating from my lower abdomen. I struggled to see; I could barely hear. The voice was odd and distorted, unrecognizable. The room around me was dark and blurred, the air cold and stark. Where was I? Who was here? Was I still in my bedroom?

Again, a painful burning sensation resonated from between my legs; a tearing, searing heat radiated into my brain.

I struggled to speak; I wanted to scream, but no sound came out. With every inkling of mental control, I pushed for my body to move. To lift. To run. Anything. But there was nothing. No response; everything was tight and locked.

Burning, pain, muffled sounds. Blackness.

***

I AWOKE AGAIN, THIS time in Uncle John's bed. I could see him sleeping on the sofa in the slight distance between us, the light from the moon faintly illuminating the room.

I screamed, my head vibrating at the sound. Uncle John jumped from the couch and raced to my side.

"Hey!" he cried, wrapping his arms around me. "Shh!"

I continued to scream, the echo of my terror and confusion reverberating around the small one-room cabin. Uncle John tried desperately to calm me.

"It's okay," he whispered into my hair before pressing his lips tightly against my forehead. "It's okay, I've got ya now."

My voice began to crack, the pressure and weight of screaming slowly fading to a cough.

Hacking and desperate for air, I pulled myself from Uncle John's arms and managed one final bellow into the night.

This time, Uncle John didn't try to stop me. He simply sat still at the edge of the bed, watching me howl toward the ceiling like a wounded wolf.

Eventually, I collapsed into a heaving clump, terrified and uncertain as to why I was here.

"It happened again," Uncle John stated, seeming to hear the rambling of my racing thoughts. "I found ya in the woods. Wet, covered in moss, rollin' around on the ground. You was screamin' again, louder than ya just did. You only make that noise when I find ya this way. The second time now. It still gives me chills whenever I hear it."

He rose from the bedside and moved to the kitchen. I could hear him fidgeting with the stove and kettle in the distance.

I looked down. I was bleeding, the sheets beneath me stained with drying blood, my nightgown soiled in a brown thickness. I screamed again.

Uncle John scrambled to my side, his eyes widening with horror the moment he saw the mass of half-dried fluid.

"Oh shit!" I heard him whisper under his breath. "Come," he said, lifting me into his arms.

Before I could recognize where we were, I felt him rising from the ground, his feet finding the front steps to the porch of the house I shared with Momma. Once inside, he lowered me into the bathtub, my stained and matted nightgown still covering my skin, and turned on the water, waiting for it to warm. The groaning and creaking of the outside water heater began to croak to life, its obvious resistance at being utilized in the dead of night clear and audible in the tiny bathroom.

Slowly, the water began to warm, and Uncle John scrubbed with fury at the visible areas of skin that were plastered with dry blood. A look of sheer panic gripped his face, a look I had never seen on him before.

Gradually, I began to calm, observing my only uncle struggle with the dried blood that clamped to my skin like paint.

"Here," he whispered, handing the washcloth to me. "You should take off the nightgown and clean yourself."

Taking the rag, I watched as he lifted to his full height and exited the bathroom, closing the squeaking door shut behind him.

Pulling my nightgown over my head, I whimpered as my eyes locked onto the site of my lower groin and inner thighs. Every last inch of skin was covered in thick, dried blood, the bright red of crimson now faded into a muddy deep brown.

Crying, I scrubbed as hard as I could, the feeling of my bare skin as it released the suction of the dried blood both painful and relieving.

Soon, the entire tub was dark with the stain of blood. I could smell the heaviness of the thickened bodily fluid as it melted and floated around me. I remained still for several seconds, once more racking my brain for the presence of memory, anything to answer the mystery of how I was once again found in the woods outside of the house. What had happened this time? What was causing me to bleed so? And from where?

I reached down into the depths of the tub, my hands resting gently on the flesh of my womanhood. Pain. It was there. That was where the bleeding was coming from, and it was caused by some form of trauma, not by my natural cycle.

I began to cry harder. I didn't scream, although I wanted to. I no longer had the strength.

After I sat alone for several more minutes, Uncle John tapped softly on the bathroom door.

"Ya okay, darlin'?" I heard him ask.

"I'm wounded, Uncle John," I cried, my tears falling faster with the sound of my voice. "Somethin' hurt me."

In the corner of my eye, I could see Uncle John's head peek in through the slightly open door, his face frowned and worried.

I continued to cry, keeping my hands pressed firmly against my intimate flesh, hoping the warm water would somehow comfort the wound and stop the bleeding.

I could sense Uncle John, his head floating in the doorway as if detached from his body. I never looked directly at him; I only continued to cry, the weight of my sobbing preventing my head from turning and blurring my vision from seeing clearly.

After some time had passed, Uncle John ventured into the bathroom, assisted me out of the water and into a fresh towel, and guided me to my bed.

The smell of the nearby pine trees filled the air the moment we stepped into the bedroom. The window was open, the faint moonlight flowing in, the aroma of the night air chilling the space.

Tucking me into bed, Uncle John moved to the window, closed it, stared out for a long moment, and then returned to the bedside.

"I'm sorry about all this, baby girl," he whispered, the faint glimmer of water wavering along his lower lids.

"I just don't understand what's happenin', Uncle John," I whispered back, my voice broken and flooded with my still-flowing tears.

"I know, sweet girl," he nodded, resting a hand over mine. "It's gotta be night terrors. It's the only thing I know of that would allow ya to venture from here and into the woods with-out ya knowin' it."

I listened but didn't agree. Something about that just didn't sound right. Something didn't connect nor feel legitimate. I simply could not believe that I would somehow manage to make it from my bed, out of the house, and into the woods. It just didn't sit right with me.

Eventually, when I started to fade, Uncle John kissed my forehead and left my bedroom. I could hear him closing the front door in the distance, the sound of his footsteps creak-ing the floorboards of the front porch, his steps eventually crunching the gravel of the pathway as he headed toward the woods that would return him to his cabin.

Placing my hands over my groin, I fell asleep in a mixture of fear and terror so intense, so alive, that it numbed every bit of my conscious mind and silenced my emotion. I simply fell into the darkness as certain and easy as a dead tree falling in the brush.

***

THERE WAS NO ONE there when I awoke this time, the sun brightly shining through my bedroom window. Slowly, the memories from the night before began to seep into my brain. First, the highness of my date with Kenneth followed by the oddness of the hazy dream, where I had heard muffled voices and felt sharp, realistic pain, concluding with the horror of waking up again at Uncle John's, the memory of moving from my bed and into the woods completely void and nonexistent.

How could this have happened to me twice? And why had I been bleeding? What had happened to me this time?

I spent the next hour slowly following my usual Saturday morning routine. Preparing a bit of oatmeal, together with a cup of coffee, I sat alone on the front porch, listening to the late-morning sounds of the Great Smoky Mountains: the chirping katydids and the various voices of the dozens of birds that filled the air with the melody of their song. Eventually, I returned to my bedroom, stripping my sheets, cognizant of the matted and stained blood that now scarred the material.

I spent the rest of the afternoon tending to the laundry, handwashing and hanging each garment, towel, and bedsheet on the house-length clothesline that lined the backside of our home. I didn't notice Uncle John watching me, until I started back toward the front porch.

"How ya feelin' today?" he asked, his face sullen, his brow furrowed with worry.

"I'm okay, Uncle John," I answered, uninterested in rehashing the details of the night before.

"Ya think we should call Dr. Reynolds?" he asked, following me up the front porch steps and into the house.

"No," I snapped, suddenly realizing the potential shame and embarrassment if Kenneth were to discover my unexplainable ordeal of night-walking and physical trauma to my intimate regions. The very thought forced me to take a seat at the kitchen table.

"I'm sorry, Gen," Uncle John whispered, moving to join me at the table. "I wish there was somethin' I could do."

"I don't wanna talk about it now, Uncle John," I said softly, my fingers trailing the lines on the old oak table. "I just wanna finish my chores and take a nap."

Nodding his understanding, Uncle John lifted himself from his chair and moved to the front door. I could see him in the corner of my eye just standing there, hesitating. It was several seconds before he finally pushed open the groaning screen door and began his journey back through the woods toward his cabin.

I could hear thunder rumbling in the distance. An afternoon thunderstorm was approaching. I watched out the window as the rain soaked the clean clothes. I didn't care to go and fetch them. I simply observed them drip with the weight of the water, their drooping soppiness as heavy as my heart.

***

SUNDAY CAME AND WENT without incident. I mostly just lay around the house, watching television and taking naps. I didn't see Uncle John for the rest of the weekend, which I found odd and uncharacteristic.

Monday's school day was just like any other. I didn't see Kenneth at all. I heard he was absent. I also didn't see Emily nor her gaggle of followers. Until after school, that is.

Just as I was heading toward the bus, Emily stepped into my path.

"Ya know ya gonna have to pay for goin' out with Kenneth," she stated frankly, Beverly and Tabitha standing on either side of her. Tabitha appeared more upset than angry, and Beverly seemed too spaced-out to really know what was even going on. After the weekend I just had, I was certainly in no mood for Emily or her stupid antics.

"Not now, Emily. I need to get on the bus."

"No," she replied matter-of-factly. "Now."

The next fifteen minutes or so remain a blur for me. The only thing I can clearly remember is knocking Emily to the ground and pummeling her ceaselessly until someone pulled me from on top of her. She had spouted something crass and vulgar about my mother, which in turn ignited my rage and sent my fists flying. A group of boys who shared my bus rides to and from school eventually guided me to where I usually sat at the back of the bus, and the usual journey home ventured forth. I don't recall much of what was said during the half-hour trip, but the entire bus was turned in my direction. Gaping mouths, frantic words, and disapproving scowls met my eyes each and every time I lifted my head.

"You're dead!" someone screamed from one of the bus windows after I had exited the vehicle and begun my trek back home.

I didn't see Uncle John in his yard when I passed, but I also didn't look very hard. I just wanted to get home and lie down for a while. I was doing just that when several cars pulled up in front of the house.

I could hear footsteps on the front porch, followed by banging on the front door. I could hear Pamela Watson, Emily's mother, yelling before I even had the chance to pull the door open.

"How dare you!" she seethed, the moment her eyes met mine. I jumped back as she fumbled for the screen door handle, her rage and fury radiating in the slight space between us. Just as she managed to pull open the creaking screen door, her husband, Emily's father, Jeffery Watson, pulled her back.

"Take it easy, Pam," he spoke softly, inching his wild-eyed wife toward the third person on the porch. I lifted my eyes to see Principal Lindsay, his powder-blue suit tailored perfectly, his brown hair neatly combed, and his bright-green eyes churning with emotion.

"We need to talk, young lady," Mr. Watson said, opening the screen door. Before I could react, he grabbed my arm and jerked me out onto the front porch.

"Just what is the meanin' of all this with hittin' my daughter?" he barked, his face scowled but his anger far less intense than that of his wife. "She's lyin' up at the county hospital as we speak."

I shook my head, desperate for a response, but found nothing but my own silence. I listened as Mr. Watson continued to yell, but was distracted by the sight of Uncle John making his way from the edge of the woods, a look of concern clearly evident on his face.

"Her nose may be broken," Mrs. Watson screamed, her voice wavering with both fiery words and gently falling tears. Principal Lindsay continued to hold her back with his left arm. I could sense that she still intended to get to me somehow. I could only imagine the rage she would unleash upon me if given the chance.

"What's goin' on?" I heard Uncle John's voice boom over the group. "Get ya hand off my niece."

Mr. Watson dropped my arm from his firm grasp, the evidence of his fingers leaving their mark with an irritated redness over my skin.

I zoned out a bit as the group of adults bickered and battered each other with angry words. From the best I could make out, I was being suspended. Or expelled. I wasn't sure. All I knew was that I was in absolute serious trouble.

"I dare not say what I really feel about this entire situation," I heard Mrs. Watson say as she slowly moved out from behind Principal Lindsay's arm. "Ya know good and well how I feel about your sister."

I looked to Uncle John, his face stern and serious as he stared back at Mrs. Watson. There was a moment of near-tangible hatred as they simply glared at each other. Finally, Principal Lindsay broke the uneasy silence.

"John," he started, clearing his throat and adjusting his dark-red necktie. "I'm afraid I just can't allow this type of violence to go on at my school."

"So, you gonna expel my niece for one little fight?" I heard Uncle John say. I was no longer able to see his face through the sea of angry people that stood between us.

"This is not the first time Genevieve has assaulted Emily," Mr. Watson chimed in, his body turned from my direction. The only person who continued to look at me was Mrs. Watson, her eyes piercing and intense. I was too afraid to meet her gaze or even turn my head in her direction. I could feel her glaring at me, and the confirmation of her angry face in my direction through the haze of my peripheral vision was enough to keep me paralyzed in place.

After another ten minutes or so of back-and-forth arguing, Mr. and Mrs. Watson departed the scene, their air of anger retreating with them. Only Principal Lindsay remained, his voice silent as he nodded and waved at the Watsons, who both stared at me as their giant, pearl-colored Cadillac lurched them forward and down the gravel driveway.

Once the debris cloud kicked up by their tires had subsided and their vehicle was completely out of sight, Principal Lindsay spoke again. This time, his voice and tone were far different than they had been while in the presence of the Watsons.

"Now, look, the both of ya," he said gently, stepping closer to the space between Uncle John and me. Slowly, Uncle John fully ascended the front porch steps, taking his place directly beside me. We waited intently as Principal Lindsay seemed to mentally prepare his words.

"I have no choice but to side with the Watsons on all this," he began, once more adjusting his necktie. "The school district can only afford so much, and if it wasn't for the Watson's generous donations each school year, there would be so much we couldn't have. Football uniforms, homecoming. Hell, even prom is completely funded by them. If I don't do what they say and expel Genevieve, they've threatened to stop all funding and..."

His words trailed into the distance, his face frozen, his eyes darting widely between Uncle John's and mine.

"Well...I just can't allow that, ya see."

He cleared his throat again, this time signifying the end of his speaking. His decision was made, and it was final. There would be no negotiating. That was clear.

"So, what am I supposed to do, Fred?" Uncle John finally responded. The use of Principal Lindsay's first name was both odd and foreign to me. "I hardly finished the fifth grade. I dropped out when I was eleven. I have no place tryin' to homeschool anyone, much less my own niece."

"I realize that, John, believe me. That's why I stayed behind. I believe I have a solution."

I zoned out again as Uncle John and Principal Lindsay discussed the future of my education. The only thing I could clearly hear was the name of Edna Stevens, the former school principal, who was now retired and living with her companion about seven miles or so from where we lived. *Companion* was the reference that was often used when describing the relationship of the two women, yet in the whispers and gossip of the townsfolk, it was widely known that Ms. Stevens and Janice Everly, her companion, were more than just living space co-occupants. Although the entire situation was still a bit confusing to me, it was said that the two women were lovers, a mortal sin openly and blatantly frowned upon and chastised by the people of Sevier County. Until I heard the rumors, I had no idea that two women, or two men, for that matter, could be lovers. It just never seemed possible to me. Yet, it also did not seem impossible. Personally, I saw nothing wrong with the matter. Who were the townsfolk of Sevierville and the hillbillies of Locust Ridge to judge? Upon overhearing Momma's telephone conversations with various female friends, the secret and private goings-on of our hillside neighbors were far less than holy and devout to the preaching or religion they so often publicly attested to. The scornful whispers and blatant judgment of two old women was both laughable if not completely asinine to me.

"I'll stop in around a month or so to see how things are goin'," Principal Lindsay said, speaking directly to me. I heard him, nodded my understanding, yet still struggled to fully grasp the reality of all that was transpiring. For whatever reason, be it emotional or simple physical and mental exhaustion, I was completely unable to comprehend the conversations that went on around me. All day in school, during the encounter with Emily, and now here on the front porch, the words of those around me transpired in warbled muffles and bubbled echoes. I had still yet to fully grasp the enormity of what was happening right before my own eyes.

A few moments later, once Principal Lindsay had slowly driven his old Studebaker down the gravel pathway toward the road, Uncle John turned his attention to me.

"What's your momma gonna say?" he asked quietly, his eyes darting over mine. "You okay, Gen? Ya been starin' around like a deaf fawn all afternoon. Are ya gettin' what's goin' on here?"

I shook my head, both up and down and side to side. I really didn't know what the hell was happening. Again, I just wanted to lie down.

Uncle John didn't bother trying to explain anything to me as he led me back inside the house, sat me down on the sofa, and turned his attention to the kitchen. Returning with a glass of orange juice and a bowl of grapes, he set them on the coffee table in front of me and simply stared.

"Go on," he urged, leading my eyes with his toward the objects he had just placed on the small table. "I think ya need to eat a little somethin'."

Obliging, I lifted a grape to my lips, slid it inside my mouth, and listened intently at the sound of the orb as it crunched and popped beneath the weight of my jaw. After several minutes of complete silence, Uncle John started to speak.

"Ya understand that you was expelled from school today?" he asked, although his tone and inflection presented the question as more of a statement. "Gen?"

I nodded, although I was still unsure as to what was really happening. My brain remained locked behind the curtain of fog that had descended it the night of my last night terror episode. Ever since waking on Saturday morning, I hadn't felt like myself. Lethargic, depressed, listless; I was completely and utterly exhausted.

"Fred—Principal Lindsay is gonna speak with Old Lady Stevens about homeschoolin' ya," he continued, his eyes heavy and concerned but his voice gentle and smooth. "That's your only hope now, Gen. Ya better pray the old lady says yes."

Eventually, Uncle John moved to kiss my forehead before disappearing out the screen door. I know he muttered something about being disappointed in my behavior, though his tone never really made me feel embarrassed nor ashamed. Perhaps I no longer had the ability to feel that way, or any way at all. I remained on the sofa, methodically popping purple grapes into my mouth one at a time, washing them down with the ice-cold orange juice.

In what must have been several hours or more, Uncle John returned, this time with his arms filled to the brim with various cloth-covered bowls, pots, and containers. He was focused on his task, and I watched from the sofa as he covered every single inch of the kitchen table with the spread. The smell of various smoked meats, some kind of bread, and various vegetables filled the small space of the living room as it rolled its way from the kitchen.

The next thing I knew, I was seated across from Uncle John, his face concerned as he stared back at me.

"Gen?" he said, his eyes labored with sudden worry.

I felt him rise from the table, but I didn't look up. I felt the weight and could smell the stench. I had vomited, all over the table, all over myself. The putrid reek of stomach acid filled the air, easily overpowering the delicious aromas of Uncle John's glorious home cooking.

Gently, he led me to the bathroom, where I watched him fiddle with the water of the tub before he urged me inside it. I didn't remove a stitch of clothing. Slowly and without hesitation, I dropped beneath the water, head and all, the warmth of the liquid both overwhelming and comforting. Perhaps I had stayed under the surface a bit too long, for Uncle John rushed to the side of the tub and pulled my upper body from below the water in one gripping, swift tug.

"Hey!" he shouted, his face an inch or so from mine. "What the hell is goin' on with you?"

I started to cry. Sob, actually. It was at least five minutes before I could manage a word, let alone a full or complete sentence. Uncle John merely held me in place while I cried, my voice echoing around the tiny bathroom with each heave and bellow of my chest. Finally, I calmed enough to answer him.

"Somethin's wrong, Uncle John," I sobbed. "I can feel it. It's like a cloud. It just drifts over me. I can't hear right. I can't think good. I'm hardly eatin', and I haven't gone to the bathroom in days. It's got me so scared, Uncle John."

For a slight second, I could see Uncle John's face wince in what appeared to be pain and sorrow. Quickly, though, he pulled himself together and hugged me against his chest.

"You'll feel better in another day or so, darlin'. I promise."

I wasn't sure how he could know that, but I trusted him. For whatever reason, I was now fully aware of the reality of my expulsion and subsequent banishment from a proper education. That subject now took the stronghold of my still-faded concentration.

"I can't go back to school?" I heard myself ask meekly, my voice as pathetic and weak as I had ever heard it.

"Well," Uncle John started, lifting me from against his chest so he could clearly see my face. "We gonna get ya somethin' else instead. I have a feelin' Old Lady Stevens will help ya out. She always liked ya momma. Ya momma was a real good student back in her day. Ms. Stevens took a likin' to her, 'specially when she found out about—"

He cut himself short.

"What?" I questioned, the focus of my brain still hazy and lost to its own fog. "Found about what?"

"Nothin'," Uncle John concluded, signaling my silence with the movement of his body. Fetching a bar of soap and a washcloth, he handed them to me, his face smiling in the yellow light of the tiny bathroom's single bulb.

"Wash up, Gen," he instructed. "Stop worryin' so much. I'm gonna go clean up the mess in the kitchen. I'll be back here in about ten minutes or so to help ya to bed. I don't want ya frettin' so much about all this tonight. We'll hash it all out in the daylight."

I didn't bother to argue with him. Instead, I took the soap and cloth and did as he asked. Once he had left the bathroom, I removed my soiled clothing and scrubbed my entire body three times over, perhaps subconsciously trying to remove both the stench of the vomit and the filth and disgust of the last few days.

I felt Uncle John kiss my forehead as he tucked in the corner of my quilt, locking me in place below the comforter. Moments later, I heard him, rattling pans and bowls in hand, exiting the front porch and crunching the gravel pathway toward the woods. I stared at the ceiling for what must have been hours, for by the time I finally fell asleep, the sound of the mountains had faded into a warbled drone and the dew of the incoming dawn now speckled over the bedroom window in countless beads.

***

THE LOG CABIN WHERE Edna Stevens and Janice Everly resided was quaint, charming, and postcard-beautiful. As if placed on the hillside direct from an Appalachian storybook, the

55

delightful farm that surrounded the cabin was both picturesque and wonderful.

I followed Uncle John up the pathway that led from the
dirt driveway to the cabin's front door. In the distance, Janice
Everly could be seen chopping wood behind the barn. She
looked up as Uncle John and I ascended the front steps of
their massive front porch.

"Well I'll be," we heard a voice exclaim. Appearing in the
doorway was Edna, her silver hair wrapped tightly in a bun,
her smiling face plump and welcoming. "Could this be young
Johnny Delany?"

Edna pushed open her screen door, moving to cup her
hand over Uncle John's cheek.

"Hey, Ms. Stevens," Uncle John beamed, his face innocent
and boyish. "How ya been?"

"Oh, honey, I'm just a'livin', I guess ya could say. The good
Lord ain't taken me home yet! Or ol' Janice out there."

Uncle John's and my eyes followed Edna's toward the
direction of the barn. Janice had resumed her woodchopping
duties, a task I had never witnessed an elderly woman perform.

"So this must be Genevieve," Edna stated, turning her
attention to me. "My, don't you look just like your momma!"

I smiled, both flattered and embarrassed.

"I hear ya got ya'self into a bit a trouble with the Watson
girl."

I nodded, keeping my head down, both in shame and
shyness.

"Well, if ya ask me, that lil' girl has a sassy mouth. Some
folks around here have told me of their encounters with her

down at her momma and daddy's store. She always has some-thin' wise or rude to say. I don't much care for that. In my day as principal, I'da taken a paddle to her backside on far more than one occasion. But, things are different now. Spare the rod, spoil the child, the Good Book says, yet so many God-fearin' people allow their children to just run amuck today. It'd never happen on my watch if I were still in charge of that school."

She laughed to herself.

"Guess it's a good thing they forced me to retire."

Heeding her invitation, Uncle John and I followed Edna inside the cabin. I couldn't get over the colorful perfection of the homey interior. Handsewn quilts adorned the walls, and neatly arranged handcrafted furniture filled most of the open areas. The small kitchen was overwhelmed with iron pans and copper skillets; the kitchen table was covered in fresh baked goods, each one competing for the aroma of the room.

"I just got through bakin' these up for the church bake sale," Edna explained as the three of us took a seat at the kitchen table. "Usually, this area is clear. This is where we'll be workin'."

I nodded when Edna turned her attention to me.

"I expect you here at seven a.m. sharp," she continued, her warm eyes now stern and matronly. "I do not tolerate tardiness, nor do I tolerate irresponsibility or goofin' off. Homework assignments will be given, and I expect them completed on time and in full. I do not take well to excuses."

Edna moved her eyes toward Uncle John.

"Just ask ya' uncle here," she laughed.

Uncle John nodded in return, his goofy, boyish smile reanimating his face.

Edna proceeded to list her seemingly endless expectations of me. I suddenly regretted clocking Emily. School was far less pressure than this. I had heard tales of Edna's strictness from both Uncle John and Momma, as well as mentions of her by various teachers throughout the years. Encountering her now for the first time, I could clearly understand why she left such a lasting impression on people.

I shook Edna's hand as we stood on the front porch, where Uncle John and I exclaimed our gratitude for both her time and selfless offer to homeschool me free of charge.

Janice had disappeared from behind the barn and was now seen riding a plow pulled by a giant mule. The sight of the elderly woman controlling such an impressive beast was both aweinspiring and comical. Uncle John and I stared for a moment before returning to Uncle John's truck.

"Ya better treat her real good, now," Uncle John commanded as we journeyed the mountain road back toward home. "I'll give ya a lift each mornin'. Please don't make me regret goin' along with Principal Lindsay's suggestion of this. Edna's a real good woman. Strict, stern, but caring. Ya have a grand opportunity here. Don't mess it up."

I nodded, keeping my gaze out the window. I was grateful yet a bit annoyed. Mostly at myself, but a bit toward Emily and her rageful mother.

I felt much better today. Clear-headed. I thanked Uncle John for the lift as I slammed the truck door shut and walked the short distance up the driveway toward my house.

I didn't see Kenneth Reynolds sitting in the corner of the front porch until I had almost moved through the front door.

"Hey," he called to me, causing my heart to nearly leap from my chest. "How ya doin'?"

"Oh my God, Kenneth," I said breathlessly, clutching my chest. "Ya scared the livin' daylights outta me."

"Sorry." He smiled, a mischievous glint sparking in each eye. "Heard ya was expelled."

I felt myself blush.

"Yeah."

"Heard ol' Emily has a fractured nose," Kenneth continued, stepping closer to me.

"Oh..." I replied, lowering my head in a bit of shame.

"Hey," Kenneth said, resting his hand on my forearm. "I like it. I think it's sexy. I like a girl who can take care of herself."

He laughed.

"Plus, it's about damn time someone put that uppity little bitch in her place."

We laughed together. I couldn't help it. Although I was ashamed and embarrassed by my violent behavior, I still believed Emily deserved it. Hell, she asked for it. No one insults my momma and gets away with it.

"Mind if I come in?" Kenneth asked, raising his eyes toward the half-open front door.

"Um..." I swallowed. "I guess so."

He pulled the squeaking screen door from my hand, freeing me to push the front door all the way open and venture inside. My heart began to beat faster as I felt him move into the space behind me. I could smell his cologne, the scent again sending a pulsating, fired sensation to my groin.

"This is cute," Kenneth exclaimed, closing the screen door shut behind him. "Charming. Quaint."

"Well, it ain't much. Nothin' like where you live, I suppose."

"Actually, our house ain't as grand as you'd imagine," Kenneth confessed, slowly wrapping his arms around my shoulders. I didn't turn around. My face was now swollen red with flushed excitement, the skin between my legs radiating and throbbing to its own pulse.

"Everyone thinks we're so rich 'cause Daddy's a doctor and all," he stated, lowering his lips to the back of my neck. "It ain't all like that. Our house is just a regular house. Nothin' fancy."

I felt moisture press against my cotton panties as Kenneth continued to move his lips down my neck and onto the tops of my shoulders. Before I could react, he spun me around to face him, cupping my face and pressing his lips to my mouth. I could taste mint as he slid his tongue over mine, the taste and sensation adding to the electricity that radiated from my womanhood.

I didn't resist when he lifted my shirt above my head, exposing my simple, plain-white bra. I didn't say a word when he lowered my jeans, pressing his lips to the front of my cotton panties. My heart beat faster as I watched him undress, the fullness of his manhood as striking and large as the ones I had seen in Uncle John's dirty magazines. The hair that surrounded it was both beautiful and arousing.

Removing my undergarments one by one, he continued to kiss my skin, lifting me in his arms and moving us to

Momma's bed in the corner of the room. I felt his lips graze across the dark hair between my legs, his tongue moving over the soft flesh below.

Before I knew it, he was inside me, the fullness of him strong and wide, the depth causing my eyes to widen, a snapping sensation radiating throughout my being.

I couldn't believe I was allowing him to make love to me. This was it: the moment I lost my innocence, my virginity. I had never seen a naked man in the flesh, never mind touched one. Yet, here I was, my legs wrapped around Kenneth's torso, watching his face morph in a mixture of pleasure and excitement as he continued to thrust his hips. In succession, we climaxed; he first, then me. My entire body shivered and quaked at the feeling. Never had I been able to achieve the same intensity in my own self-induced orgasms. My fingers nor Uncle John's pornography could ever touch me or make me feel the same way as Kenneth could. Lying together atop my mother's bed, our naked bodies adhered to each other with sweat, I focused on the scent of his flesh, the smell of his cologne, and the feeling of the course hair that encased his manhood, which was now pressed tightly against my leg. Before I could utter a single word, we made love again, this time Kenneth twisting and altering my body into various poses and positions. When he climaxed again, he gently bit the corner of my neck. The feeling of him pulsating inside me led me to my own finish.

***

THE MEMORY OF THE last few days melted and fizzled beneath the warm bath water as I laid my body against Kenneth's. The sensation of his naked skin below mine was so arousing; I could feel the warmth of my tender flesh even underneath the heated covering of the liquid. We laughed and joked, talked and kissed. Never in my entire life had the tiny bathroom been a place I never wanted to leave. I felt Kenneth slide inside me again as we made love in the tub. He tugged at my hair as he lifted and lowered my backside against him. The sound of the water sloshing and spilling over the side of the cracked porcelain accented our moans as we finished together.

"I think I'm fallin' in love with you," Kenneth whispered in my ear as I rested my head back against his naked chest.

I smiled, my face full and hot with blood, both from the sex and my excited embarrassment.

I couldn't help but stare at Kenneth as he dried himself. The lines and bulges of his muscular, athletic body moved and glistened in the soft afternoon light as he gracefully and methodically dried his skin. My heart skipped a beat as I watched him move the towel through his pubic hair and over his manhood. The tender flesh of the organ flopped and bounced from side to side as his hand journeyed from his groin, down his thighs, and toward his calves and feet. The view of his strong backside was just as arousing as his front, with the sight of his manliness dangling between his legs.

Lifting me from the water, Kenneth gently and lovingly dried my body, pressing his lips to each section of flesh he carefully moved the towel over. I closed my eyes and rested my head on his shoulder as he carried me to my bedroom.

There, he slowly untucked his towel, exposing his erection, and leaned forward to meet my naked flesh on the bed. It was then we heard footsteps on the front porch. I scrambled for a nearby pair of slacks and T-shirt, while Kenneth bolted to the living room. His erection waved and slapped his skin as he ran for his randomly tossed garments. Hastily dressed, I entered the living area to see a half-clothed Kenneth frozen and staring at Uncle John.

My heart fluttered as Uncle John's eyes moved from Kenneth to me, his expression shocked and seemingly traumatized.

"Wha—" he croaked, his head bouncing between us.

"Hey, Mr. Delany," Kenneth managed to say as he quickly concluded the rest of his dressing.

Uncle John only stared.

Kenneth moved to the sofa, where he put on his shoes, tied them, and then slowly inched around Uncle John and managed a way through the screen door, off the front porch, and into the beyond. His car wasn't here. He must have walked. My heart jumped a bit as I realized Kenneth had trekked miles just to see me. I could still smell his scent on me: the smell of his skin, the scent of his cologne, the sweet tanginess of his saliva.

"Gen..." Uncle John whispered, his expression falling from shock to sadness. "Why?"

I moved toward him, now able to see the tears welled in his eyes.

"Uncle John, I'm sorry, but—"

Uncle John spun around and threw open the screen door. The old wooden door slammed against the frame as I watched him bound off the front porch and take massive strides toward the woods. I didn't see him again for the rest of the day.

***

THE VIOLENCE OF THAT night's hazy nightmare was far more brutal than the ones that had come before it. I could hear a voice. The sound was deep and gruff. I couldn't make out the words. I didn't understand a thing. Shapes and shadows surrounded me. The cold of the air pricked at my flesh and stung my senses. I was naked; I was on my back. The pain from my lower regions was excruciating and constant. Over and over. Back and forth. Shadows moved. Sounds droned and echoed. Pain. Burning. Pain.

***

I WOKE UP SCREAMING. I was in my own bed, but my nightgown was on backward. I could sense the presence of someone or something leaving the room. My panties weren't completely around my thighs. I could feel warm blood, this time seeping from both the front as well as the back. I could move, but my head was foggy and weighted. My vision was still blurry, although I could clearly make out the overall detail of my bedroom.

I groaned as I lifted my entire upper body with both arms. To my horror, my legs would not move. They would not respond. I could not feel them. What was happening? What was going on? I felt dizzy. I dropped myself back onto the mattress, my head thudding hard against the pillow. I drifted back into the shadows of the night.

***

"GEN."

A voice broke my slumber.

Slowly, I opened my eyes and lifted my head. I was in exactly the same position I had been in when I had awoken the last time: still on my stomach, my panties slightly lowered. I snapped my head around to see Uncle John standing in the doorway of the bedroom, his back to me, his face turned to the side. It was clear he was trying to avoid looking directly at me.

Tugging at the length of my nightgown, I turned over, relieved that my legs now responded to the signals from my brain, dropped my feet to the floor, and inched toward the dresser.

"We have to leave in ten minutes if we gonna make it to Edna's on time."

I nodded, although I knew Uncle John could not see me.

Rushing around, I managed to dress, wash my face, tie my hair back, and make it into Uncle John's waiting truck in less than the allotted ten minutes. Uncle John and I did not speak during the entire truck ride to Edna's. The air was thick and uncomfortable between us. To say that the atmosphere was awkward would be more than an understatement. The shame and embarrassment I felt after Uncle John caught Kenneth and me together had faded to the terror and nightmare of the hours that followed. I decided it was best not to mention any of it to Uncle John. Not because I was still ashamed and

65

embarrassed, but because I felt it was better not to worry him with further detail regarding my ongoing night terror issue.

"I'll be back to pick you up around three," Uncle John said as I was sliding myself from the truck seat and onto the gravel of Edna and Janice's driveway. I nodded, flashed a nervous half-smile, and slammed the truck door shut. I stood in silence, watching Uncle John's truck disappear beyond the distant tree line.

"Well, good mornin', sunshine," I heard a voice behind me say. I turned to see Edna, standing behind the screen door, a steaming mug of something hot gripped firmly in her hands. "Would you like some coffee? Tea?"

"No, ma'am." I smiled, inching my way toward the front porch.

"Is everything okay, sweetheart?" she asked, squinting her eyes through the screen that stood between us.

"Yes," I replied meekly, nodding my head in agreement.

"Very well, let's get started. We have a very long day ahead of us."

Around noon, Edna stopped our lessons, which had been focused on history and a bit of math, two subjects I absolutely despised, and moved to the kitchen to prepare lunch. I remained seated at the kitchen table, lost in the daydreams of my mind.

"Hon," Edna called from the nearby icebox. "I know I'm doin' all this for free, mostly because I always enjoyed your mother back when she was a pupil of mine, I respect Principal Lindsay, and your uncle has always been nothin' but a fine young man as far as I am concerned, but I am not goin' to wait on ya hand and foot. Get ya'self in here and help me with this lunch."

Embarrassed, I moved to assist, joining Edna on a sandwichmaking assembly line. There were three plates, so I assumed Janice was most likely going to be joining us.

As if on cue, Janice entered the cabin the very second Edna and I set the table with the sandwiches, glasses of fresh apple juice, and silverware. Sweaty, hot, and a bit smelly, Janice took her seat at the table, directly across from Edna, and began to munch on the corner of her chicken salad sandwich. She must have felt me staring, for she turned her head in my direction, mouth open, half-chewed food showing, and stuck out her tongue. Gasping, I didn't know how to react, but felt semi-relief when Edna began to laugh, which cued Janice to join her. I felt my face flush as my eyes darted between the two women. Like gleeful schoolchildren causing mischief at the cafeteria lunch table, both were in their own world of in-the-moment joy and playful humor. I couldn't help but smile.

Janice didn't say too much as Edna filled the lunchtime with stories of her days as principal of Sevierville High School, she and Janice's trip to the Carolina coast, and her concern over the current political climate of the nation. The war in Vietnam was certainly something that angered her passionately. Both Janice and I had long finished our meals when Edna finally concluded her self-professed rant.

"I'm gonna go nap out in the hammock," Janice announced as she lifted herself from her wooden chair and into a slightly bent stance.

"What time did ya come to bed last night?" Edna asked, gathering debris from the table and into her arms. Taking her movement as a hint, I jumped from my chair and began to help.

"Just a bit after midnight," Janice replied, adjusting the straps of her worn and tattered overalls with her claw-like, dirt-covered hands.

"Watchin' for the lights again?" Edna asked, shuffling toward the sink. I followed her, only half-listening to their conversation.

"Not watchin' for...watchin' 'em."

"You saw 'em again?" Edna asked, spinning around to face Janice, the handful of dishes still tucked between her arms.

"Yup, they was standin' still just northeast of here. They didn't move for about an hour...then zipped off like they was never even there."

I froze. They were talking about the moving stars, the same ones I had seen just weeks prior, flitting and zipping over the woods between my house and Uncle John's cabin.

"You talkin' about the movin' stars?" I asked, softly lowering the dishes I had collected into the large porcelain sink.

Both Edna and Janice stared at me.

"I've seen 'em too. One time. A few weeks back. They moved around like hummingbirds. Zipping here, flitterin' there. Then...poof. They vanished."

Janice pointed at me. I stared back at her, suddenly nervous, but felt a bit of relief when she eventually spoke.

"See, Edna," she said, still pointing. "Even the girl has seen 'em. I told ya I wasn't goin' crazy."

Edna stared at me, her mouth slightly agape. "Well, I'll be," she said softly, turning her head back toward Janice. "Fine, fine," she said, finally moving to deposit her armful of dirty dishes. "There are flyin' lights above Locust Ridge. I guess I believe ya."

"They ain't just lights," Janice continued, moving toward us in the kitchen. "They men from outer space."

Edna started to laugh as she turned to face Janice, but her laughter ceased once she caught sight of her face.

"I seen 'em myself."

Edna and I could only stare, the feeling in the room suddenly dark and heavy.

"Ya know what I'm talkin' about, Edna," Janice continued, her wrinkled face rising with the movement of her bushy eyebrows.

"What on earth are you babblin' on about, Janice?" Edna asked, sounding annoyed, moving back to the kitchen table to continue clearing it. Silently, I followed her, although my mind was completely focused in anticipation for what Janice would say next.

"I seen 'em in the woods. Several times now. Short ones. Some tall. They all got eyes like grasshoppers. They don't say much. They just stare. But I seen 'em, and I know they seen me."

I felt a chill move down my spine and through the entire length of my arms. I could sense Edna becoming a bit nervous.

"Alright, Janice, enough of that now," she scolded, flashing her eyes at me and then back to Janice. "Ya gonna scare the girl."

I started to cry. I couldn't say why or for what reason, but I fell into the chair I had been sitting in earlier, my tears heaving my chest into a fit of sobbing.

"Oh my...what's the matta, darlin?" Edna cooed, moving to my side. I could hear her knees groan and crack as she lowered herself beside me.

"I've been havin' these night spells," I confessed through wet, tearful sobs. "I don't know why or what's happenin', but they been goin' on ever since I first saw those lights."

In the corner of my eye, I could sense Janice approaching. She tugged at Edna's sleeve, signaling for her to move. I could smell the deep musk of her sweat and skin as she lowered herself in the place Edna had just been.

"What kinda night terrors?" she asked, her breath ripe with the smell of chicken salad and chewing tobacco.

"I don't know, just these weird dreams. And I've woken up a few times in the woods. I don't ever remember it, but my uncle finds me out there...screamin'. That's happened twice now, and just last night, it happened in my room."

I could hear Edna gasp. Janice moved closer, gripping my forearm.

"Have ya seen the men in the woods?" she asked, her few yellow teeth glimmering in the dim light between us.

"No," I whispered, shaking my head. "I've only seen the lights. And only one time. I thought they was stars."

"Okay," Edna interrupted, assisting Janice to her full height. "I'm stoppin' this right now. No more. I don't wanna hear another word about these lights or little men in the woods.

This girl is here for an education, not a lesson in Janice Everly scare stories."

Janice didn't respond. After a brief moment, she shuffled past the table and began to head for the screen door. I felt her staring at me before she exited onto the front porch. In that instant, I could feel that she understood me. She heard more words than I was speaking when I detailed what I could recall of the night terrors. I couldn't wait to get her alone. For whatever reason, I felt she had more of the answers I had been silently seeking.

Edna dismissed me from the table five minutes to three. With a handful of notebooks and textbooks, I bounded off the front porch and toward one of the various shed-like buildings that surrounded the cabin. I found Janice inside one of them, silently collecting chicken eggs from a wall full of wire cages.

"The men are vistin' ya," she said, without looking up. "Don't say anything to Edna, but that's what's goin' on. They been here before."

I could feel my blood racing through my veins, a tinge of fear and sheer terror vibrating along the wires of my nerves.

"What do ya mean *vistin'*? What do they want?"

"You, hon," she said matter-of-factly, never looking away from her methodical egg collecting.

"I—"

My voice was broken by the sound of Uncle John's truck horn.

"What can I do?"

"Nothin', child," she responded, her voice firm and solid.

"But...Janice...please. I'm scared."

Gently placing the now full egg basket atop a nearby wooden crate, Janice moved in my direction, her dirty and withered face lined by the light of the afternoon sunlight that peeked into the coop through the spaces between the wooden boards of the walls.

"Just don't fight 'em," she whispered, standing directly in front of me. "There ain't no way to stop 'em. They always get what they after."

"Gen!" I heard Uncle John shout in the distance.

"Go on," Janice directed, nodding her head toward the waiting truck. "Just don't fight 'em."

Before I could say another word, she moved from the coop and toward the barn. I could hear her chopping wood as I slowly walked toward Uncle John's truck.

"You okay?" he asked the moment I slid onto the truck's sole bench seat. "You as pale as a ghost."

"I'm fine, Uncle John," I whispered, feeling a cold sweat bead across my brow.

I could sense Uncle John staring at me, but he didn't say another word. Instead, he tossed the old engine into drive, and we journeyed down the gravel pathway toward the dirt mountain road that would lead us home.

***

I WAS FAR TOO terrified to sleep. Instead, I lay on my back, fully clothed, staring at my bedroom ceiling for what felt like hours. I eyed the faintly illuminated nightstand alarm clock as I lifted myself from the bed and moved to the door. It was five after midnight.

The sounds of the night swarmed around my head the moment I stepped off the front porch. Crickets and various other insects battled for the top tier of the symphony each of their cricking legs or chirping mouths contributed to. Moving mostly by memory, I followed the worn-out pathway that led from the side of the gravel driveway and into the woods that would take me to Uncle John's cabin. The sky was cloudy; I couldn't see any stars. The only light was from that of the moon, which was dim and overcast by the billowing veil of the fast-moving clouds.

The crickets grew louder and the other night bugs sounded clearer as I moved further into the complete blackness of the gathered trees. The sound was so overpowering that I couldn't even hear my own footsteps, even less my own breathing or heartbeat. Suddenly, there was a person. I could sense them. Someone was standing right in front of me. I could feel them breathing in the slight space between us. I felt my heart race, my skin prickling with fear. I started to scream, but the presence moved, ran. I could hear the muffled sound of the footsteps pounding over the soft dirt of the wooded pathway.

Too terrified to move, I remained still, the swirling sounds of the night bugs flocking around my head. Finally, after what seemed like hours, I dared myself to budge, following the sound of the now distant running footsteps toward Uncle John's cabin. Just as I moved from the tree line, I heard the firing of a car engine and saw the faint-red taillights of a vehicle as it skidded its way toward the nearby road.

I started running, moving from the edge of the woods and onto Uncle John's front porch in record time. I didn't bother knocking; I burst through the door, taking in the dimly lit scene before me. Habitually, I closed the door behind me, though my thoughts were nowhere near the forefront of my mind. Slumped over the side of the couch was Uncle John, a large stainless-steel syringe glimmering atop his forearm. Rushing to his side through the faintness of the dying kerosene lamp, I could see the silver of the needle where it protruded from one of his veins. He wasn't moving, although I could hear him breathing. His mouth was open, but his eyes were closed.

"Uncle John!" I screamed, shaking him. "Uncle John!"

***

THE SUN WAS JUST beginning to peek out above the nearby treetops when Uncle John finally opened his eyes. Observing the room for a moment, he jumped to his feet, looked around the couch and surrounding floor, and then lifted his eyes to mine. I could see fear, panic, and shame drifting over his expression the longer he stared at me.

"Why ya here, Gen?" he asked plainly, his voice void of the emotion I could so clearly see on his face.

"What's goin' on, Uncle John?" I asked, holding up the syringe I had pulled from his arm just hours before.

He only stared, not at the needle in my hand, but directly into my eyes.

"Put that down, Gen," he said calmly, slowly adjusting his clothing and moving toward me.

"What is this, Uncle John?" I demanded, my head dizzy and spinning from lack of sleep and overall emotional and psychological pain and fear. "Why was this in your arm? What's it for?"

"It's for pain, Genevieve," Uncle John stated as he moved close enough to snatch the syringe from my grasp. "It's medically prescribed. I'm not some junky. I've needed it for years. It's a private matter. It's not your concern."

"I don't believe that, Uncle John," I confessed, unblinking as I stared back at him. "You was slumped over. Passed out. I don't believe this was prescribed by a doctor."

"Believe what ya want," he concluded, moving past me toward the stove. "But that's what it's for."

"I'm gonna tell Momma," I whispered without thought and more to myself than to him.

Before I could blink or utter another sound, Uncle John grabbed me by my wrists, his fingers over my skin tight and painful. His breath reeked of hours of drug-induced unconsciousness as he barreled his words into my face.

"You mention a word of this to your momma and I'll kick your ass, little girl," he threatened through clenched teeth. "The last thing I need is for her to be over here in my business. I do what I agreed to. I watch after ya. I make sure ya ain't gettin' yourself into any trouble."

He hesitated, stepping back, letting go of my arms.

"But apparently, I ain't watchin' close enough. You and that boy. I know what you was doin' just before I walked in that day. I can't believe it, Gen, a little slut just like—"

He stopped, darting his eyes over my face.

"Just like what?" I asked, warm tears streaming over my skin. "Just like Momma?"

"I didn't say that," he sighed, moving back to the stove.

"But that's what you was gonna say, isn't it?"

He began to prepare his stovetop percolator. The smell of fresh coffee grinds filled the air the moment he opened the steel container he kept them in.

"Say what you was gonna say, Uncle John."

"I ain't sayin' another word, and that wasn't what I was gonna say anyhow. That woman is my sister. I ain't gonna talk that way about her to nobody, much less her own damn kid. Now get ya ass home and get ready to go to Edna's. I'll be there in half an hour."

Still crying, I slammed the cabin door shut, jumped off the front porch, and ran into the woods. The memory of encountering the mysterious stranger along this very same path crept into my brain as I treaded heavily toward the other side of the dense collection of trees. I didn't want to think about it. I didn't want to concern myself with something I could never know the answer to. Between the chat of strange men in the woods, lights in the sky, someone on the pathway, and now Uncle John with a needle stuck in his arm, I was certainly in no mood to think, sit, ponder, relax, sleep, nor even eat. I dashed into the house, changed my clothes, splashed cold water over my face, and walked toward Uncle John's waiting truck, ready and willing to face yet another hectic day.

***

I DIDN'T SEE JANICE for the entire day. I got the sense that Edna, still upset and disturbed by the conversation from the day before, had perhaps told her to steer clear of us. Tired, weary, and uncaring as to a negative reaction, I finally asked about Janice's whereabouts, just before Edna had dismissed me for the day.

"She's feelin' under the weather," Edna announced after a slight moment of staring. "She's lyin' down."

I nodded, knowing full well it wasn't the truth. I had peeked in at the two women's bedroom earlier in the day, when Edna had excused herself to the outhouse. Unless Janice was lying down in the chicken coop or barn, she wasn't here.

I waved goodbye to Edna as I jumped into Uncle John's truck. My head was light and spinning with exhaustion. I could not wait to get home so I could finally sleep.

Just as we were nearing the entrance to the gravel driveway of my house, Uncle John stopped the truck, tossed it in park, and cut the engine.

My heart skipped when he scooted toward me, placing one hand over mine, and one on my shoulder.

"Listen here," he said, both sternly and comfortingly. "I have an old work injury that never quite healed." He kept his eyes fixed firmly over mine. "Dr. Reynolds makes house calls to me. He keeps me up to date with pain medication. It's all under his care and advisory. I don't want ya to mistake what ya saw."

I could feel my heart beating in my throat as I listened. I wanted to believe what he was saying, but I just didn't.

I decided it was best to just nod in agreement and change the subject.

"There was someone in the woods last night," I stated. I could feel Uncle John looking at me as he reignited the engine and we ascended the path of the driveway toward my house.

"What do ya mean?" he asked.

"I was walking through the woods toward your place a bit after midnight, and I came upon someone walkin' my way. I didn't see who it was. They didn't say anything, but there was definitely someone there. I could sense them there. I could feel them breathing."

Uncle John stopped the truck just before the front steps of the porch.

"Don't worry about it. It was probably just a deer."

I laughed. "Yeah, a deer that can drive a car?"

I saw a faint flash of panic pale Uncle John's face.

"I'm sure it was nothin', Gen. Why don't ya just get inside and do whatever homework Edna assigned ya."

I nodded and exited the truck.

Uncle John didn't speak another word as he lifted his foot from the brake and turned the old truck back toward the mountain road.

Tossing my schoolwork onto the kitchen table, I kicked off my shoes, unfastened my overalls, and stripped down to my bra and panties. I fell onto the bed, and it took only seconds for me to drift to sleep, the swirling sounds of Uncle John's lies echoing in the memory of my ears.

***

"SO..." EDNA STARTED, NERVOUSLY fidgeting with her freshly sharpened pencil.

It was Friday afternoon, our last day together for the week. I hadn't seen Janice since the day she joined us for lunch; I really wasn't sure where she was, and I felt it was best not to ask Edna about it.

"This has been a productive week," Edna continued, tapping the pencil against her open notebook. "You're a fine pupil, Genevieve. I'm glad I agreed to do this. It's a shame you are no longer allowed to learn with your peers, but at least you will be finishin' your education. I mean, who can go wrong with one-on-one learnin'?"

I smiled and nodded in agreement.

"I need to ask ya, though," she began again, nervously gulping from her coffee mug, "that talk about the night terrors and all...was that true?"

I was suddenly nervous, the waver in Edna's voice signaling my anxiety over the subject.

"Yes," I whispered, keeping my eyes focused on the open science book that occupied the space on the table before me.

"Have ya told your momma about them?"

"No," I answered, shaking my head. "I haven't seen Momma in a while. I'm hopin' she'll be home this weekend."

"Ya need to tell her, dear. This is somethin' important a mother should know about her child. Especially if you are venturin' outside the house and whatnot."

I nodded.

"Now," she started again, this time finishing off the contents of her mug, "the talk about lights in the sky and mysterious men in the woods and all..."

I felt her place a hand over mine. I looked up to meet her sympathetic gaze.

"I don't want ya worryin' about all that nonsense. That's just somethin' Janice likes to go on about, but there ain't nothin' to it. It's all just a figment of her imagination. She means well, but it's part of the reason why she's seen as an outcast. Well, that and..."

I continued to stare as Edna lowered her eyes to the table.

"Because you two are lovers?" I heard myself ask, the sound of my voice surprising even me. I didn't mean to say it. I was instantly mortified that I did. Much to my relief, Edna looked up at me and laughed.

"Well, I don't know about all that these days," she chuckled. "We're old biddies now, but, yes, at one time, for many years, we were very much lovers. Today, we tend to just look after each other, mostly. When ya get up in age like us, those feelin's and urges tend to fade away. Hell, it's a blessin', really. Too much youth is spent, male and female, chasin' around a means to an end based off hormones. Don't get me wrong, love and lovemakin' are beautiful, wonderful things. Blessin's from God. But, boy howdy, can they lead ya into a world of trouble. I'm relieved to be rid of it all."

She lowered her eyes again, a bit of pink blushing her cheeks.

"Well, for the most part, that is."

I laughed, I suppose a subconscious attempt at easing the older woman's sudden embarrassment.

"I understand, Ms. Edna. I'm sorry for bein' intrusive or outta line."

"Oh, no, darlin'. You ain't outta line at all. Besides, I know you've heard the gossipin' and rumors about us from the townsfolk and other mountain people around here. People have always found the two of us and our arrangement a bit strange. Hell, I'm sure I would too if I wasn't a part of it. But Janice and I have somethin' special. Somethin' that's always been beautiful. Somethin' that many people go their whole lives without experiencin'. I'm grateful for it, and I wouldn't trade any of the hardship or hurt we've endured because of it for anything in the world. Janice has been my whole life these past fifty years, and I know I'm exactly where I'm supposed to be. This farm."

She paused, her eyes lifting dreamily into the distance.

"With her," she concluded softly.

"Anyhow, back to those night terrors. Don't let her scare ya that they have somethin' to do with the stories she makes up about these little men from Mars or wherever. What you are experiencin' is serious. Dangerous, even. Ya need to let your momma know about 'em. Perhaps she needs to take ya to see Dr. Reynolds about it."

I grimaced. Again, the thought of Dr. Reynolds knowing of my nightmare episodes was simply too close and too connected to Kenneth for me to chance or risk. No, my issue was best kept at home, between Uncle John and me. Perhaps I would tell Momma about them when I saw her, but it would depend on her mood, her ability to listen, and most of all, her understanding. I really didn't want to bother nor concern Momma with something she couldn't do anything about, let alone have her worrying about me every night from her motel room miles away in Gatlinburg.

"What made ya bring them up, anyhow?" Edna continued, slowly pulling her papers together into a neat pile. "I mean, what made ya think of 'em during the talk of the lights and little men and all?"

I shook my head.

"I don't really know. It just sorta came out. For some reason, hearin' what Janice was sayin' made sense and seemed to connect to this mystery about myself I've been carryin' around and tryin' to ignore. I guess it all just seemed to fit together, is all."

"Well, it doesn't, honey. And I don't want ya goin' around thinkin' you're bein' visited by strange little people from another planet. Ya got somethin' else goin' on, and ya need to have it looked into. By a professional. Promise me you're gonna tell your momma about all this."

She paused for a moment.

"Well, minus the movin' lights and mysterious little men in the trees part, that is."

I smiled, nodding. "I promise, Ms. Edna."

I listened half-heartedly as Uncle John and Edna chitchatted about the weather and toll it had been taking on their crops. Edna and Janice lived mostly off their farm, much in the same way Uncle John did his. Store-bought foods or goods were a rarity in their homes, besides basic items such as coffee beans, various medicines, and perhaps some canned spices. Their vegetables were grown in their open fields, and their poultry, pork, and beef came from their own livestock or that of neighboring farms they bought and sold or bartered and traded with.

Uncle John was quiet on the way home as was I. Still tired from all that had been going on lately, I decided it was best not to burst the bubble of discomfort that surrounded us with the sound of mindless and useless chatter. I waved goodbye as Uncle John descended my driveway, and I drudged into the house like a horror film zombie without a brain. Just as I was closing the front door, I heard a voice half whisper my name.

I turned to see Kenneth creeping toward the front porch steps from the side of the house.

"Kenneth," I whispered, darting my eyes toward the driveway to be sure Uncle John had fully disappeared from view. "What are ya doin' here?"

"I needed to see you, beautiful." He smiled, stepping up the front porch steps. He too turned his head toward the end of the gravel driveway. "Is your uncle comin' back?"

I felt my heart jump in both excitement and worry.

"I don't know, Kenneth. It's possible. He comes and goes from here often. I never know when he might show up. I don't think it's a good idea if ya—"

Kenneth pulled me to him, locking his lips over mine. Before I could move or utter a sound, he slipped his tongue beyond my lips, swirling it around the inside of my mouth.

I closed my eyes, the feeling of Kenneth so close to me igniting the electricity of the lower extremity of my being. I could feel the fire of arousal starting to spread over every inch of my skin, both exposed and private.

"No," I whispered, pulling my head away from his. "We can't risk gettin' caught again."

Kenneth smiled coyly. "Come then," he said, pulling me down the front porch steps and into the backwoods behind the house. Together, laughing, we raced hand in hand to the nearby train tracks. I was amazed that the same buzzing I had experienced during my last visit to the tracks returned with equal intensity. The sound and vibration brought me to my knees.

"Are you okay?" Kenneth shouted after I broke from his grasp and fell onto one of the steel rails of the track.

"Yeah," I answered, gripping the backside of my head with both hands. "There's just this weird headache I get whenever I come near these tracks."

I could feel Kenneth staring at me, an awkward silence befalling the atmosphere around us.

"Come on, let's get ya up."

As soon as I joined Kenneth on the wooden center of the railway, I was fine. It was only the steel that seemed to irritate the sound. Together, once more hand in hand, Kenneth and I journeyed the distance of the train tracks toward Sevierville, all four hours worth. The time seemed to slip by without notice. I couldn't believe that we made it into town as quickly as we did. Due to the back-and-forth conversation between us, the time it took to venture from the woods behind my house and into Sevierville felt like it transpired in no more than twenty minutes or so. The pleasure of Kenneth's company was so all-consuming that not a thought nor care of worry entered my brain the entire time we were together.

"Let's go eat," Kenneth declared as we approached the track's crossing in the heart of Sevierville.

Silently, I followed the pull of Kenneth's hand as he led the way up Main Street and to the sole café that rested at the north end of the town's busiest street. Various heads turned and onlookers paused when we entered the small doorway of the café.

My heart sank the moment I locked eyes with Emily Watson. Sitting beside her: Barbara Bishop and Tabitha Paul.

"Come," Kenneth said softly, placing himself behind my back and guiding me with his hands. The eyes of the three girls appeared to penetrate my flesh as Kenneth led me to a nearby table for two. I could feel them staring, their glares relentless, but I refused to look in their direction. Kenneth did the same. Instead, we continued the conversation we had been enjoying during the walk along the tracks and allowed the world around us to fade away into a sound-warbled blur of sightless abandon. It was only when Tabitha Paul approached the table that we broke from our unified distraction.

"I just want the two of ya to know that I am not jealous of this," she declared, pointing between Kenneth and me. "I've moved on. Bobby Boyd's asked me out. Ya know, the quarterback."

"He's actually the lineman, but okay. Good for you, Tabitha."

Tabitha's face twitched at the sound of Kenneth's voice and words. Apparently, his declaration of the true sports position of her newfound beau was both infuriating and insulting.

"Fuck you, Kenny," she hissed, slapping the top of Kenneth's head with an open hand. "Enjoy your whore."

Kenneth grabbed her arm before she could walk away.

"Apologize," he commanded. "Now."

Tabitha turned her head in my direction, smirking and scoffing.

"No, Kenneth. I ain't apologizin' to the daughter of a tramp… who is apparently followin' right along with her whore momma's footsteps."

I started to lift from my chair, but Kenneth stopped me.

"Apologize, Tabitha. Now! Or I ain't lettin' ya leave."

Sitting back down from the light press of Kenneth's hand, I toured the now silent room with my eyes. Every single patron of the café was now frozen and staring.

"I don't have to listen to you, Kenny!" Tabitha laughed. "I'm through with ya!"

Pulling herself from Kenneth's grip, Tabitha returned to her table, signaling for her two gawking friends to rise and follow her.

"Whore!" they shouted as one voice, laughing amongst themselves as they scurried out the door of the café. Again, I started to rise from my chair, and again, Kenneth stopped me.

"Leave it be, Gen," he said gently. "They ain't worth it."

It wasn't until we shared a milkshake together that I felt my nerves and anger subside to the explosive rush of sugar that now invaded my veins. Staring into Kenneth's eyes and laughing at his corny jokes, I was in love with every single second of this moment. How could I be so lucky as to win the attention and affection of the town's most handsome and sought-after high school bachelor? Every girl at Sevierville High must be envious, most of all Tabitha Paul and her two evil best friends. I didn't care though. I didn't really have to see them anymore anyhow, and after the last explosive encounter with Emily, she appeared to keep her distance. I am sure the last thing she wanted or needed was a public display of humiliation if I were to once more pummel her smug face with the anger of my fists. There was never a time I was going to let her get away with insulting my mother, and she knew it. I wouldn't be the least bit surprised if she had encouraged Tabitha to approach our table, perhaps somehow hoping the encounter would escalate into something physical, to both distract and take the tinge off her own encounter with me. Everyone in town knew I beat her down the last time. It was a scar to her tough-girl, all-American town princess reputation that she so haughtily and gracelessly protected.

The sun had long set by the time Kenneth and I returned to the tracks. We were nearly halfway through the second half of our second hour of the journey, when a bright orange light started to glimmer in the distance.

"What is that?" I whispered at Kenneth, his face frozen with concern. "A train?"

"Nah," he answered, squinting his eyes for a better view. "They stopped this route a few years back. No engines run this rail anymore."

"It looks just like the sunset," I chimed in, nervously locking my hand in his. "I'm gettin' a little scared, Kenneth."

"It's okay, Gen," I heard him say just as the light seemed to lurch toward us. In an instant, the orange glow moved down the track at a seemingly impossible speed. One minute, it appeared miles in the distance; the next, it was less than a quarter mile or so in front of us.

There wasn't a sound, only the deep orange glow of the light. It was featureless. I couldn't tell if it was round or rectangular. It was just an orange glow, hovering over the entirety of the train track.

"Let's get off here," Kenneth urged, pulling me over the steel rail. The moment my foot lifted over the steel beam, I fell onto my stomach, the vibration and ringing so intense and powerful that I became completely deaf to the world around me. I could see Kenneth moving his mouth as he bent forward to help me from the ground, but I couldn't hear him. The only sound my brain could process was that of the massive, vibrating hum. What was worse, is it sounded as though it were coming from inside my own head, not from some external source.

Just as Kenneth began to lift me from atop the steel, the orange glow became yellow, moving closer. The feeling of the glow could be felt by the skin as the mass of light inched nearer. I had to squint my eyes. The intensity of the brilliance rivaled that of a midday sun. I could feel Kenneth pulling me, but my body didn't seem to move. I couldn't hear him, but I knew he was yelling. I could feel his body vibrating and heaving from the force of his voice and movement of his breath. The last thing I remember was the feeling of being completely engulfed by the light. No more Kenneth. No more railway. No more vibration. Just light.

***

IT WAS COLD WHEN I opened my eyes. Above me, the tangling of tree branches rose toward the night sky. I could see the stars glowing brightly behind the blackened hieroglyphics of the fingerlike tree limbs.

My head hurt; my legs were aching. My breasts felt sore, and the back of my neck felt burned and raw. Where was I? What had happened?

Just as my mind began to piece together the last puzzled moments of my final seconds of consciousness, I heard voices in the distance. I waited. I listened.

"Genevieve!"

It was my name. There was more than one voice. As they continued, they sounded closer, one of them sounding more familiar and distinct. Yes. It was Uncle John. One of the voices was certainly Uncle John's.

I tried to call out. To yell; to scream. Even to open my mouth, but I was still too frozen and aching among the fallen dead pine needles of the forest floor. Finally, I was able to lift my head, noting that my shirt was only half on. My jeans were open and unbuttoned but pulled in place atop my thighs.

Slowly, I worked my way into a stance, the sound of my voice breaking free the second I could stand to my full height.

I screamed, a scream so loud that it vibrated the side of my head. I even felt like I could sense the odd vibration that would haunt me whenever I was near the steel lines of the railroad tracks. I wasn't sure, but it didn't matter anyway.

Then, it all came to me: walking the tracks with Kenneth, the feeling of being overcome by the light.

Before I knew it, two pairs of feet were standing at my side. I lifted my head to see both Uncle John and Kenneth, their faces pale and their eyes wide with worry.

"Oh my God, Gen," Uncle John sighed, pulling me into his chest. "We've been lookin' for ya for hours."

I could see Kenneth over Uncle John's shoulder, his face filled with fear, his eyes darting wildly around the surrounding woods.

"What happened?" Uncle John asked.

I shook my head. "I don't remember." I looked to Kenneth. "I just remember a light."

"See!" Kenneth said, pointing, moving his eyes toward Uncle John. "I told ya. It was a light. It just took her."

Uncle John peered back at Kenneth, his face stern and suspicious.

"So, you sayin' a light just made a grown girl disappear into thin air?"

Kenneth darted his eyes back to mine.

"Well—" he swallowed, so hard that the sound could be heard feet away "—I don't know. I think I got knocked out or somethin'. But what I remember is pullin' on Genevieve, then she was gone. I came to next to the tracks. She wasn't there. And it's taken us this long to find her."

He moved his eyes back to Uncle John's.

"And look how far she is from the tracks."

Both Uncle John and I looked around us. It was true; the tracks were nowhere to be seen. I had no idea where we were, but the train tracks were most certainly nowhere in sight.

"Let's get her outta this cold," Uncle John said, rewrapping his arms around me. "You and I will discuss this further once we get her home."

We walked at least a mile before we broke through the trees and onto the dirt roadway that would lead us home. The moon was bright above us, but even in its most brilliant of stages, it could not rival the intensity or overwhelming power of the light Kenneth and I had encountered earlier. Whatever it was, it was like nothing I had ever experienced before in my life.

Uncle John led me to my bedroom once we were inside the house.

"Get in your nightgown, Gen," he directed, pulling back my quilt to expose the bedsheets. "I'm gonna go talk with Kenneth."

I simply did as I was told. In the distance, I could hear the two male voices bickering, arguing back and forth about the possibility of a strange light, my disappearance, and the hours that had apparently transpired before they were able to find me.

I didn't care about any of it. I pulled the blankets and quilt over my head and sank into the endless blackness behind my eyes. The constant buzzing behind my ears was still present, lulling me to sleep.

****

MOMMA WAS IN THE kitchen when I awoke the next morning. I smiled when I saw her but was disturbed by her expression when she laid her eyes on me.

"What's goin' on?" she asked breathlessly, dropping her half-consumed cigarette onto the kitchen table and moving to embrace me. "Uncle John said you was lost in the woods last night. What happened? Why was ya in the woods at night?"

"Momma," I whispered, "I—"

"Talk to me, Genevieve," she shouted, pulling me from her chest so she could see my face. "What's the matter with ya? Ya know not to leave outta this house after dark!"

I shook my head in both confusion and frustration. It was obvious that no matter what I said, I was most certainly not going to get through to my mother at this time. She was scared, and her maternal fear was so intense and tangible, you could practically wrap your arms around it.

Eventually, Momma calmed into a puffing chimney of visible anxiety. Finally, I felt I could explain.

I started with the night terrors, detailing each one as they remained in my memory. I didn't hold back a thing. I mentioned the fear, the pain, and the bleeding. I moved the story to the final episode, the one before the lights on the train track. I told Momma of how I had woken up with my panties around my thighs, the stranger I had encountered in the woods, even the needle I had found in Uncle John's arm. I knew he would be livid that I told her, but I just had to. I couldn't stop the enormity of the flow of words that gushed from my mouth. Weeks, days, and hours of mystery, fear, and terror unfolded from my tongue as clear and vivid as I could possibly make it. Momma sat paralyzed, her face frozen in a scowled expression of fear and panic.

"Oh my God," she finally whispered, her final drag of cigarette smoke escaping her nose and mouth simultaneously. "What is happenin' to my baby?"

I saw a tear fall from her left eye as she scrambled from her kitchen table chair to my side. Together, we lay on her bed, the rhythm of her sobbing both comforting and alarming. Finally, she lifted her head to speak, locking her eyes over mine.

"I'm movin' ya to the motel," she announced, nodding her head in agreement with her own words. "Ya can't stay here no more. Not with this goin' on. Ya haveta come back to Gatlinburg with me."

"Momma, no," I argued. "I gotta finish my studies. Ms. Edna is gonna—"

"Ms. Edna?" Momma seemed confused. "What're ya doin' with Ms. Edna?"

"Oh..."

My words sank to the floor as I realized I was also going to have to detail the events that had led to my expulsion from school. Perhaps deservingly, Momma struck me with an open hand after I had finished revealing the entire situation. I could feel her sadness and disappointment in the sting of her slap.

"What about Uncle John, Momma?" I eventually asked, the powerful force of her open hand still vibrant and hot across my cheek. "He needs help. I need to be here for him."

"Your uncle is a drug addict, Genevieve," Momma replied very matter-of-factly. "He's been a morphine addict for years. Don't ya ever wonder why he never leaves to go to work? Why he's always there on his farm, in his cabin? He spends his nights as high as a kite. It's been this way since you was a girl. He don't need anyone but his own junky self."

I could feel in the fire of her words that she no longer wanted to discuss Uncle John. Instead, she lifted herself from the bed, moved to the kitchen, and began tinkering with our old percolator. Within minutes, the aroma of freshly brewed coffee suffocated the entire house.

I sat with Momma at the table, the two of us sipping the hot, black liquid, Momma lighting yet another cigarette.

"I'm gonna talk with Ms. Edna," Momma finally stated. "I'm gonna see if she will allow ya to just stay over there for a while. At least until I can figure somethin' out."

"But, Momma, I'm fine here. It's just—"

"Ya ain't fine here, Genevieve. Someone is doin' somethin' terrible to ya! Wakin' up in the woods. Wakin' up bleedin'. Your panties down. How is that fine? That ain't fine! That's the furthest thing from fine, Gen. That's fuckin hell!"

I winced at my mother's use of profanity. By no means was my momma a well-spoken individual, but she was always ladylike enough to never use strong obscenities; at least, never in my presence.

"We'll go to Edna's in the mornin'. I leave on Monday. First, I need to go and handle some things with your uncle."

Momma finished her cigarette, sucked down her final drops of coffee, and headed out the screen door. She didn't return for nearly two hours, and when she did, her face was beet red, her eyes swollen. It was obvious she had been crying. Sobbing, even.

I tended to my regular Saturday chores per usual, consciously giving Momma her space in the house. That night, we sat together on the sofa as we had done so many times before, laughing and chatting excitedly at the hours of programming that led us into the wee hours. I slept beside her on her full-size, corner-of-the-room bed. When I opened my eyes, it was daylight, the sounds of the morning birds clear, the stream of fresh sunlight beaming in through the various windows. I didn't wake her; I simply watched my momma as she slept, a woman still in her early thirties, her face lined and wrinkled with the trauma of pain and worry. It felt as though I were peering into my own future, the weary and fading beauty of my mother a crystal-ball-like glance into the reflection of what was to come for me.

***

"WELL I'LL BE," EDNA exclaimed as Momma and I exited Momma's old and worn powder-blue Buick. The vehicle harbored countless miles, its constant trekking between Gatlinburg and Locust Ridge possible and held together by the likes of Uncle John's handiness and mechanical abilities. Many times, Momma's old car wouldn't make it beyond the edge of town, causing Uncle John to have to jump in his truck to go and assist her, Momma calling him from some mountainside farmhouse or gas station she had to walk miles to find. I was more than curious about the discussion that had transpired between my momma and Uncle John, but I knew it was best not to pester Momma about it. Certainly not now anyway. As soon as she awoke this morning, she bathed,

95

dressed, and rushed me to get ready so we could venture to Edna's.

"Could that be little Ms. Eva Delany!" Edna exclaimed as we neared the front porch. "I haven't seen you in nearly twenty years, dear girl! How are ya?"

I smiled and watched as Edna, or Ms. Edna as I always called her, threw open the screen door and embraced my mother with a mighty and long-lasting hug. The two women chitchatted excitedly about the last time they saw each other, before moving on to discuss memories of their shared time at Sevierville High, with Momma as a student and Ms. Edna as her principal. Mentioning various names of teachers and students, their conversation was so energetic and enthusiastic that one could not help but beam while witnessing it.

Finally, after what must have been more than half an hour, Ms. Edna invited us inside for coffee. Momma didn't detail the reason for our visit for at least another hour.

I excused myself to the outhouse as Momma tearfully described her fear and worry for me regarding the ongoing night terrors and whatnot. I really didn't want to hear the conversation, much less re-witness my mother's obvious and overwhelming pain and worry, so I felt it was best to just go and sit on the open hole of the wooden board of the toilet seat, waiting until I had not only emptied my bladder, but also given what I assumed would be enough time for the two women to discuss my future living arrangements. It was when I exited the quaint, clean, and charming outhouse that I saw Janice, her back turned to me, her withered hands busy with a hammer and nail on the side of one of the various shed-like buildings. She knew I was there long before I neared her.

"I hear you is movin' in here," she said as I closed the distance between us, standing just a foot or so behind her shoulder. "Another visit from the strange men?"

I shook my head, somehow knowing Janice could see it, even though her attention remained fixed on the hammering task before her.

"Why is your momma all frantic, then? What happened?"

"Well, there was another episode. But this time I was awake before it happened. It was on the train tracks, the one for the old route that runs through Sevierville. I was walkin' along it with Kenneth Reynolds, when a strange orange light approached us. It got real bright and yellow...almost like the sun. It threw Kenneth off the side of the tracks. We both woke up, and the light was gone. I was way off in the woods some-where. It took my uncle and Kenneth a few hours to find me."

Janice continued to hammer as though she were no longer listening to me.

"That was them, alright," she finally remarked. "They movin' in fast on ya now. Not carin' who's around to witness. I'm not sure if it's a good idea that you stay here."

I felt my brow furrow in confusion.

"Why do ya say that?"

"I don't want those things comin' back around here. It took me long enough to scare 'em off the last time. If that's what even happened. But they don't come around here no more. I just see their lights now. I guess they found what they was lookin' for."

She concluded her hammering, dropped the tool into a tin bucket beside her rubber work boot, and turned to face me.

"You, darlin'. They found you."

"Genevieve!" I heard my mother call from the cabin. Janice smirked and walked off. She had disappeared before I could even manage a thought or sound. Reluctantly, I returned to the house.

"Let's get back home and pack some things. Ms. Edna has agreed to let ya stay."

I looked from Momma's face to Ms. Edna's eyes. Ms. Edna smiled back at me, her eyes moving from mine back to Momma's.

"Now, since she is doin' so much for us, you'll be given a list of daily and weekly chores to handle. I don't wanna hear any fuss or hear of any backtalk or laziness, ya understand?"

I nodded without thinking. I didn't look away from Momma. I simply returned her gaze, just agreeing with everything she said. The last thing I wanted to do was disturb or upset her.

I gave Ms. Edna a hug, and she kissed my cheek before I followed Momma from the front porch and back to her old Buick. In the mirror on my side of the car, I could see Janice approach Ms. Edna on the front porch, and the two women appeared to start arguing. The last sight I saw before Momma turned the corner at the end of the gravel driveway was Ms. Edna throwing her hands up dramatically and returning to the inside of the cabin, leaving Janice, who had now turned in the direction of our quickly disappearing car, staring with a frozen frown locked over her expression.

***

"DON'T WORRY ABOUT UNCLE John," Momma commanded as she helped me fill various duffel bags, paper shopping bags, and plastic trash bags with my belongings. From the depths she was reaching into my tiny closet, it was clear that I was not going to be returning home for quite some time. Nervously, I continued to fold a stack of underwear, placing them neatly in the corner of one of the bags as Momma slammed various coats, blankets, shoes, and even my sole black dress that I wore to rare weddings and funerals into one of the duffels.

With nearly my entire life packed into Momma's car, we moved down the driveway toward the road, when Uncle John stepped out from behind the nearby trees.

"Where ya takin' her?" he yelled at the windshield, standing firm in front of the car.

"Get outta the way, John!" Momma yelled, angrily pressing the steering wheel car horn.

Hesitantly, Uncle John stepped aside, allowing Momma to punch the accelerator and fly past him in a cloud of gravel-covered debris and dirt.

Momma didn't speak during the entire car ride back to Ms. Edna's. Until we got there, that is.

"Listen," she spoke softly, taking my hands in hers. "I don't want ya contactin' your uncle for the time bein'. There are things I need to discuss with you about him, but for now, I just want ya to settle in here with Ms. Edna and Janice, make yourself useful, keep polite, and tend to your schoolwork. Don't let him distract ya, and don't worry about Emily Watson or those little friends of hers. I'm gonna take care of all that.

You just sit tight here until I figure out what I'm gonna do motel-wise."

I wanted to argue with her, but I knew it was best to just keep my mouth shut.

"Do ya understand, Genevieve?" she asked after several seconds of silence.

"Yes, Momma," I whispered meekly, the sound of my voice sunken and pathetic.

I could see Janice out behind the barn, what looked like a pipe hanging from her lips. She glared back at me, her eyes deep and penetrating even in the long distance between us. She must have been angry, for Ms. Edna informed me that for tonight, at least, I would be sharing the bed with her until another arrangement could be made.

Momma announced that she would be returning to Gatlinburg tonight instead of Monday, and that she would be calling in a few days to check in. I could tell she was still determined to somehow get me to Gatlinburg with her, a thought and prospect I dreaded and feared even more than my night terrors.

I spent the rest of the afternoon and evening assisting Ms. Edna with various household and outdoor chores. Janice never came around. In fact, it would be several days before I would see Janice again, and when I did, I would most certainly wish that I hadn't.

***

"SHE HAS TO GO," Janice exclaimed, bursting through the screen door, causing both Ms. Edna and me to jump in place. We were in the middle of a social studies exam; the house was quiet as Ms. Edna was busy grading my homework from the previous evening and I was completing an essay for the exam.

"Janice, wha—"

"Save it, Edna. I'm sorry, but the girl has to go. I understand she's in a bit of a situation, but there ain't nothin' we can do to stop what's happenin' to her, never mind help her. I'll help pack her things, but she has to go tonight."

"Janice, stop!" Ms. Edna shouted, standing from her chair. "Go back to the barn. I've already warned ya about comin' around here when you're in one of your states. Unless ya can pull yourself together, ya need to stay away from both Genevieve and me."

"That girl's brought 'em back!" Janice screamed at the top of her lungs, her eyes wide and wild, her dirt-covered finger aimed in my direction. "I saw 'em last night. They kept back at the edge of the woods, but they was here. They is waitin' and watchin', and they will come here if we don't get her away from us!"

"Out!" Ms. Edna matched the height and urgency of Janice's voice. "Out until you calm down!"

I watched in a stunned state of disbelief as the two elderly women pushed and shoved each other. Janice eventually obeyed Edna's command to leave the cabin. Muttering to herself, she pounded her rubber work boots over the wooden floorboards and kicked her way out the screen door.

"They comin'!" she yelled as she rounded the side of the house. I could feel myself begin to shake in what I could only describe as panicked nervousness.

"Hey," Ms. Edna cooed, witnessing my distress. "You just ignore all that. Don't take a word of it to heart. Ya ain't goin' nowhere. You're stayin' right here with me as agreed upon with your momma. Janice...well, Janice isn't well, hon."

"What if she's right, Ms. Edna?" I heard myself ask in a whisper, my voice seeming to work all on its own. "What is she seein', then, if what she's sayin' it is ain't true?"

"Lord knows, child," Ms. Edna answered, shaking her head. "Janice has a history of seein' things that ain't there. For nearly a decade, she was seein' leprechauns...or trolls, I don't remember. Whatever it was, she went on and on all frantic as she is now. Swearin' they was stealin' from our crops and harmin' our animals. Hell, she even had me out there in the night watchin' for 'em...but ya know what? Nothin'. Never saw a thing. It was all nothin' but the workin's of a sick woman's wild imagination."

Ms. Edna took her seat.

"I've loved that woman for such a long time now, but the love has changed. It changes every day. She's become more of a sister in need in these most recent years. I hesitate to say burden...but..."

I nodded my understanding, a subconscious effort to try to ease the obvious pain and worry of the old woman sitting before me.

"Now," Ms. Edna continued, wiping her face of a few rogue tears, "get yourself back into that social studies exam!"

***

MOMMA CALLED TO CHECK in the next day. I didn't mention Janice's episode. I just told her about my recent schoolwork, confessed that I was indeed helping around the house and farm, and listened as she revealed the details of the hopeful move we would make together to Gatlinburg. She said she had even spoken to a Sevierville real estate agent about selling the house. My heart sank as I listened, but I never said a word in response.

Perhaps it was the water or Ms. Edna's cooking, but I was starting to become nauseous more and more. Nearly every morning when I awoke, and always after lunch, I would find myself vomiting or retching in the outhouse. I kept it from Ms. Edna. I didn't want her worrying. I figured it would go away after a few days. I had suffered these minor bugs before, on my own back at home, many, many times. They always tended to pass with time.

***

IT WAS SATURDAY NIGHT when the sound of a shotgun caused me to jump out of a deep sleep. Surprisingly, Ms. Edna remained still and peaceful next to me. Obviously, the same sound had not affected her whatsoever.

Carefully and quickly, I snuck out of the cabin and into the yard. It was a dark night, no moon, only a canopy of diamond-like stars. I could hear movement in the distance. It was coming from the barn. Creeping ever so quietly, I inched closer, slowly able to make out the hazy and dimly lit sight of Janice reloading a shotgun.

"Janice!" I called as I drew closer, afraid that any surprise may cause her to fire in my direction. I wanted her to know I was there before any sudden noise spooked her or she sensed my presence before I had the chance to announce it.

"Watch out!" she screamed in the same piercing pitch she had used in the house a few days prior. "They there! They there!"

I ran. I didn't think. I just ran. I didn't know what was where, but I most certainly made it from the yard and into the barn in just a few quickened strides. Janice pulled me close to her once I was near enough to reach. The barn was eerily lit by a wall-side torch. From what I could see, this area of the building was Janice's loft. There was a small twin-sized bed, mattress frame and all, a tiny table littered with various tools, utensils, and dirty dishes, and even a bureau, which, from what I could see, was plastered over with newspaper shreds and clippings.

"Did ya see 'em?" Janice whispered, still fidgeting with the shotgun.

"No, Janice, I didn't see anyone. Don't ya think Ms. Edna would be upset if she knew you was out here shootin' that gun like that?"

"Edna's ignorant. She's blind to what's right in front of her. She's seen 'em too. She just won't admit it. Like so many people, she just puts it outta her mind. She forces herself to forget. But deep down, she knows. She knows they here. And she knows they is comin' back because of you."

"Janice, please, I—"

She held up her hand, signaling my silence.

"Listen," she whispered, pointing toward the back of the barn.

The other side of the massive wooden structure was solid black. I couldn't see a thing. The light from her wall-side torch was faint and flickering. As much as I tried, I couldn't make out any detail of the other side of the barn.

"Hear 'em?" Janice asked in a whisper. "They just along the tree line. They know you is in here."

I felt a chill move along my upper body. As ridiculous as all this was, Janice's passion and energy for the subject was affective and influential. I couldn't help but feel just a bit terrified.

It was then that I heard it: a sharp, slightly piercing cry. It sounded almost like a wounded animal. Something predatory. A wolf or panther, perhaps.

"I think that's just an animal, Janice," I whispered, my body inching closer to hers.

"That ain't no animal, girl," she replied, lifting the shotgun, aiming it toward the back of the barn. "That's them. They talkin' to each other. They know you is in the barn."

I didn't know what to say. I didn't know what to do. Of course, I didn't believe a word of what this woman was saying, but I was also now too deeply involved to simply run from the barn. I felt she might shoot me if I moved too quickly or did anything to attract what she felt was so close by, watching, waiting, and hell-bent on capturing me.

Just as Janice perfected her aim, the same vibrating ring echoed from behind my ears and to the front of my skull. It must have been the barrel of the shotgun. Like the steel of the train tracks, the black metal of the weapon must have influenced the same effect on whatever it was that caused the ringing. Suddenly, there was a flash, a bright, blinding white light that filled the barn from floor to ceiling. The ringing in my head intensified, and I fell to my knees. Then, just as quickly as it had begun, it was all over. The light, the ringing. After what felt like minutes, Janice finally crouched at my side.

"They gone," she said calmly. "Good thing I was here, child, or else they surely woulda taken ya."

I didn't look up. Instead, I focused on my breathing, intending to follow the rhythm of my lungs into a state of inner calm.

"Genevieve!" a voice could be heard yelling in the distance.

"Come," Janice commanded, grabbing my wrist and lifting me from the floor.

Shotgun in hand, Janice kept a firm grip on my arm as she led me back in the direction of the cabin. Darting her eyes over the heavens, I could hear her mumbling to herself as we moved. Ms. Edna was waiting for us on the front porch.

"What the devil?" she exclaimed the moment her eyes hit the gun. "Janice...wha—Gen?"

She darted her eyes between Janice, the gun, and me, trying desperately to understand what her eyes were showing her.

"It's okay, Ms. Edna," I chimed in. "Janice thought she heard a coyote out near the pigs. I came out to see if she needed me to go with her."

Janice was still gripping my arm. She didn't dispute what I said, but she also didn't verbalize nor display any physical form of agreement. Ms. Edna just continued to stare. I don't think she believed me, but it sufficed her worry for the time being. After dismissing the shotgun-wielding Janice back to the barn, Ms. Edna led me back inside the cabin.

"Sit," she commanded, pointing to my usual seat at the kitchen table. "I'm gonna make ya some tea. Ya need to warm up a bit. Out there in this night air like that. I swear…"

I started to feel sick and attempted to make it out the back door and toward the outhouse, but I was too late. A putrid stomach bile slid over my tongue and onto the floor of the cabin. Ms. Edna was at my side within a second or two.

"Oh dear," she said gently. "Are ya sick, hon?"

I nodded. "I think so. I've been throwin' up a lot lately."

Ms. Edna didn't respond. Instead, she quickly wiped the floor with a nearby rag and assisted me to my feet.

"Sit," she directed.

Returning a few minutes later with a fresh mug of ginger tea, Ms. Edna pressed the back of her hand to my forehead.

"No fever," she concluded, watching as I slowly began to sip the tea.

"How long has this been goin' on?"

"All week," I confessed. "I didn't wanna say anything. I didn't wanna worry you."

She pursed her lips and squinted her eyes. "How often does it happen?"

"Off and on. Mostly in the mornin' and right around lunchtime."

Ms. Edna's eyes wheeled, but her lips remained pursed and sealed. "I see," she finally mumbled, returning to the kitchen.

We chatted mindlessly for the next half hour or so, finally returning to bed after we had both consumed a cup of tea and visited the outhouse.

I could feel Ms. Edna staring at the back of my head as I drifted off to sleep. I wasn't sure why, but I had a funny feeling that there was far more going on inside her mind than she was alluding to.

***

"WAKE UP, HON," MS. Edna said softly, slowly pulling back the large handsewn quilt that covered me. "Dr. Reynolds will be here within the hour."

I jumped from the bed and into a complete stand, my eyes wide, my breathing labored.

"Wha— why?" I started, but the sickness ceased my words and forced me to run from the cabin. I only made it halfway to the outhouse when another batch of the same rank bile slid over my tongue and through my lips.

"This is why he's comin', child," Ms. Edna whispered, catching up with me. "He agreed to make a house call after church."

I didn't bother saying another word or attempting to argue. I knew there was nothing I could do to stop the plan that had already been set in motion. Instead, I relieved myself in the outhouse, washed my face, brushed my teeth, and dressed. I sat at the kitchen table, a bowl of oatmeal before me, a glass of orange juice beside it. I didn't touch them. I was far too nervous and nauseous to even begin to think about food.

I heard a car pull up and two voices fill the air. There was a man's voice, I presumed Dr. Reynolds's, and Ms. Edna's.

I could hear their conversation as they drew nearer to the front porch.

"No, I didn't call you here for Janice, Doctor. I have another matter I'm tendin' to."

I listened as Ms. Edna briefly detailed the situation of me coming to stay with her, the agreement with Momma, and the details of the various night-terror episodes. I hadn't seen Dr. Reynolds in years, but I recognized him the moment he appeared in the kitchen. To my surprise, he peered at me suspiciously, almost knowingly, as if he knew something about me no one else did. His expression and demeanor made me immediately uncomfortable.

"Hello, Genevieve," he finally spoke, following Ms. Edna to the table. "I hear you're havin' some sick spells. Vomiting."

I nodded, still uneasy by the look in the man's eyes. Despite my sudden discomfort, a part of me was drawn to him. He looked like Kenneth, or Kenneth looked like him, I should say. Both were handsome, with dark eyes, perfect hair, and chiseled features. I could smell the same cologne Kenneth wore as the doctor moved closer. I assumed they shared the same bottle.

"Let's have a look at ya, then," he said gently, placing his black leather medical bag on the table beside him. Ms. Edna pulled out a chair for him to sit on, and he began to examine me.

His hands were hard and cold as he moved them over my skin. His palms were clammy, and he was slightly shaking. He seemed nervous. The entire ordeal made me highly uncomfortable.

"Okay, I have to ask ya a few personal questions," he finally spoke after concluding the movement of his hands over nearly my entire body. "Are ya a virgin, dear?"

I felt myself become dizzy. I had to sit back down. Ms. Edna was just behind me, resting a hand on my shoulder.

"Um…"

How was I going to admit to this man that I had had sex with his son? Several times, in fact. Did he know Kenneth and I had been seeing each other? Would he be upset by it? What would Ms. Edna think if she heard that I was no longer a virgin?"

"It's very important ya tell the truth, dear," I heard Ms. Edna say gently from behind me.

I shook my head, lowering it to my chest. It was a clear enough signal to provide a definite answer.

"Ya may be pregnant," Dr. Reynolds announced. "When was the last time ya had your period?"

My mind started to scramble. Flashing images of my night terrors, the sex with Kenneth, and my physical altercations with Emily all tumbled into my brain at once. I couldn't distinguish one from the other, and I most certainly couldn't remember the last time I had my period.

"It's alright," the doctor whispered, resting a hand over mine. "We'll find out soon enough. If the sickness continues and she misses a cycle, please call me, Edna. For the time bein', just as a precaution, take it easy. Continue drinkin' the ginger tea."

He presented a bottle of pills from his shiny leather bag. Ms. Edna snatched them up and carried them off to the kitchen. Momentarily alone, Dr. Reynolds just stared at me, an uncomfortable, odd look circling his eyes. What was he not saying to me?

I remained seated as Dr. Reynolds and Ms. Edna said their goodbyes. Ms. Edna returned to the table the moment the doctor had driven his car off the end of the property.

"You can tell me the truth, dear," she said lovingly as she sat in the chair Dr. Reynolds had been sitting in. "Who's the boy?"

I told her everything. All about Kenneth. I didn't go into graphic detail, but I made it clear that we had made love, and more than once. Ms. Edna just listened, her eyes divulging no judgment, no disappointment.

"You're becomin' a woman," she finally stated after I concluded my honest confession. "I'm not sure if Dr. Reynolds knows he's soon to be a granddad, but that will be a bridge we will all have to cross in time. For now, let's just follow his orders and keep ya rested. Schoolwork as usual tomorrow. Mother-to-be or not, you are still my pupil, and I still have a responsibility to get ya fully educated. It's the greatest gift you could possibly provide for yourself and your future child."

I sat alone on the front porch later that evening, slowly moving the old hanging swing with my feet. Watching the sun as it moved behind the tree line, I thought of my life, what was and what I presumed was to come. I had never once thought of the possibility of being pregnant. I mean, of course I knew how it all worked, and Kenneth and I were certainly not careful nor preventative in any way, but for whatever reason, I had never once even considered the thought that my sickness could be caused by a new life growing inside me.

At bedtime, I lay beside Ms. Edna, the deafening sounds of the Smoky Mountain night air accenting the ceaseless train of my thoughts. What was Momma going to say when she found out I may be pregnant? How was I going to afford raising a baby? Perhaps I should live with Momma in Gatlinburg. Maybe she could get me a job at the motel as a maid or something. Whatever was to come, I wasn't fearful, just nervous. I fell asleep to the sound of one particular nearby cricket, his chirp and tone off beat with the others and higher in pitch.

***

THE NEXT MORNING, MS. Edna had me urinate into two small clay pots. One was filled with a handful of barley seeds, the other, wheat seeds. She said it was an old pregnancy test. If the wheat sprouted, I was having a girl; if it were the barely that sprouted, it would be a boy. If neither sprouted, I wasn't pregnant.

I found the entire ordeal to be embarrassing, disgusting, and ridiculous, but I went along with it anyway. What harm could it do? Ms. Edna set both pots out on the front porch, just beneath the chain-link-held wooden swing.

"Ya know," Ms. Edna began, closing her notebook, the visual signal that the school day had ended. "Dr. Reynolds never once mentioned your night terrors. I told him about them when he'd first arrived. I wonder why he didn't ask ya any questions in that regard?"

I shrugged, uncaring and uninterested. The last thing I wanted to do was talk about the strange occurrences I had experienced both inside and outside of my own home. It was bad enough that Dr. Reynolds knew I was potentially pregnant. I could only imagine what he had said to his son.

Later that evening as the three of us sat at the kitchen table for dinner—Janice had been welcomed back inside the cabin, her rants and spells of seeing the men in the woods had apparently ceased—we heard a truck pull up in front of the house. Ms. Edna excused herself to the front porch. I looked at Janice, who didn't seem to notice what was going on. She picked and pulled at her meat and cornbread as if it were the last meal she was ever going to enjoy. She was back in the bed with Ms. Edna at night; I had been commissioned to a small cot in the living room. It wouldn't take much for Ms. Edna to expel Janice back out into the barn though. One wrong word about lights in the sky, strange visitors in the woods, or talk of me leaving would be grounds for re-banishment. The sound of Ms. Edna's raised voice broke me from the distraction of my thoughts.

"Get outta here, John!" I heard her cry over the sound of a resistant male voice.

"She's my damn niece!" I heard Uncle John shout, the sound of his voice moving closer to the cabin. Before I could react or even move, he appeared in the kitchen, his face unshaven, his hair wild and disheveled. He looked like he had been wearing the same clothes for days, and from the large, blueish bags that rested beneath his eyes, it appeared he hadn't been sleeping very much, either.

"Gen," he whispered, falling at my side. "I've been worried outta my mind about ya."

"Hey, Uncle John," I replied meekly.

Ms. Edna stormed into the room.

"John, ya better leave now, or I'll be forced to call the sheriff!"

"Calm down, Edna," he shouted, his face becoming scowled with anger and frustration. "I just wanna talk to her."

Clicking her tongue in obvious disapproval, Ms. Edna disappeared from view.

"I'm sorry for not lookin' after ya better," Uncle John continued, his voice wavering with visible tears, his breath heavy with the tinge of his homemade moonshine. "I shoulda stopped what was happenin' to ya."

"The night terrors?" I asked, lifting my hands and placing them atop my uncle's wild and disheveled hair. "Uncle John, what could ya have done? They're just nightmares."

"But they ain't, Gen," he sobbed, lowering his face onto my lap. "They ain't just nightmares."

"What...I don't under—"

"Leave. Now!"

Ms. Edna reappeared in the kitchen, Janice's shotgun in hand.

Uncle John turned his head in her direction, nodding his approval.

"Please," he begged Ms. Edna. "Please, shoot me. I deserve to die."

"Uncle John!" I cried, pulling his face back in my direction. "Stop talkin' like that! Right now! I won't allow it. You didn't do a damn thing."

"That's just the reason, Gen." He sighed. "I didn't do a damn thing when I coulda done everything to stop it."

Without warning, Ms. Edna aimed the gun toward the back door and fired a shot through the screen.

My ears rung, both from the echo of the gunshot and from the internal, vibrating buzz that seemed to be initiated by various forms of metals.

Heeding the warning, Uncle John leaned forward, kissed my brow, lifted himself from the floor, and exited the room. Ms. Edna followed him, reloading the shotgun as he passed her.

I spent the rest of the night trying to figure out and understand what Uncle John had been trying to say. What could he have possibly done to stop my night terrors? He did all he could by rescuing me from the woods when I would awake there screaming at the top of my lungs. Was he too talking about the strange lights and mysterious men Janice had been seeing? Was something extraordinary, or even otherworldly, happening to me? It took me hours to fall asleep, but when I finally did, my slumber was fraught with endless tossing and turning due to nightmares and visions of what these mysterious men must look like. The terrifying image of a slender being with large, grasshopper-like eyes filled the space behind my eyes, waking me from a dead sleep. I struggled to catch my breath as I rose from the cot. The vision had been so vivid, so clear, I was certain I had seen in real life what my brain had just unconsciously shown me.

***

AFTER TWO FULL WEEKS of nothing but morning sickness, near sleepless nights, and ongoing pangs of overwhelming nausea, it was quite certain that I was indeed with child. To my surprise, the wheat seeds had sprouted inside the small clay pot Ms. Edna had planted them in. The barley seeds remained below the soil. As far as Ms. Edna was concerned, there was no longer any doubt in the matter. Not only was I pregnant, but I was also having a girl. I did accept the fact that I was carrying a child; my monthly cycle had seemingly stopped altogether, but I wasn't quite sure if I believed the old wives' tale regarding the sex of the child or not. Aside from my schoolwork and household chores, I spent most of my days obsessing over the future. I had started to become very nervous about divulging my pregnancy to Momma. I also had begun to wonder what Kenneth knew and how I was going to tell him if his daddy hadn't already. A week later, I got my answer.

Kenneth Reynolds pulled up in front of the cabin just after sundown on a Friday evening. I had just finished washing the dinner plates from supper and was preparing to work on some unfinished homework. Ms. Edna waited to greet him on the front porch.

"Well, hello there, Mr. Reynolds," she said plainly as Kenneth rushed from the car and toward the front porch. "I'm glad to see ya. I know ya don't really know who I am, but—"

"Oh, I know who ya are, alright," Kenneth confirmed, cutting Ms. Edna off. "Where's Genevieve?"

Listening from the kitchen table, I could hear Ms. Edna scramble to gain control of the conversation.

"Hold on just a minute," she started again. "I have a few things I'd like to say to ya first."

"I ain't interested in hearin' 'em," Kenneth replied, his footsteps pounding on the front porch steps. "Now, are ya gonna invite me in, or am I just gonna have to barge in uninvited?"

Ms. Edna didn't say another word, and after a few seconds or so, the sound of the screen door could be heard opening and slamming shut. I looked up to see Kenneth standing in the doorway.

"Gen," he said softly. "Oh my God, I been goin' crazy lookin' for ya."

I smiled nervously.

"Hey, Kenneth," I managed to squeak.

"I had to practically threaten your uncle with death just to get your whereabouts from him. He didn't wanna tell me, but eventually, he finally did. Especially when I threatened to get my daddy involved."

"Ya mean your daddy didn't tell ya I was here?"

Kenneth looked confused. "Why would my daddy know where you was?"

"Because he was out here doin' a checkup on me just three weeks ago or so. I figured he woulda told ya."

My words appeared to stun Kenneth. I could see the thoughts behind his eyes as they spun wildly.

"Was ya sick or somethin'? What's goin' on, Gen? Why'd ya momma bring ya here?" His eyes darted around the room. His face sank into a frown of disapproval. "Here with these sinners?" he concluded.

Before I could say a word, Ms. Edna appeared behind Kenneth.

"If that is how ya feel, young man, and if that is how you are goin' to choose to behave, I'm gonna have to kindly ask ya to leave my house," she stated calmly, her eyes watered and wide.

Kenneth moved his eyes from Ms. Edna over to me. I just stared back at him. There was nothing for me to say. Honestly, I was surprised by his response, and a bit hurt and annoyed at his rudeness. He must have read the thoughts etched over the disappointed expression on my face, for he turned his head back toward Ms. Edna, smiled, and apologized.

"Now, I still would like to say a few words," Ms. Edna stated, nodding in my direction. "But for now, I think you two have a lot of talkin' to do."

She didn't wait for a response from either Kenneth or me as she turned her back to us and exited the room. The screen door could be heard opening and closing in the slight distance. A few seconds later, Kenneth and I were completely alone.

I opted to invite him for a walk. Hand in hand, the two of us ventured along the outskirts of the farm property. The handful of livestock: a milk cow named Pasadena, a pen full of pigs, and the clucking hens in the nearby chicken coop, all vocalized their awareness of our presence as we neared and passed their allotted homes on the farm. Pasadena mooed loudly when she saw me, perhaps expecting me to feed her, which was one of my daily farm tasks. I waited until Kenneth and I were nearly to the tree line before interrupting the awkward silence between us with some of the answers to his list of questions. At this point, I decided it was best just to be completely honest with him. I briefly detailed the handful of night terrors, Momma's fear and decision to move me to Ms. Edna's for protection, from what, I still wasn't sure, and of course, the new discovery of my pregnancy. I could feel Kenneth's hand go cold the moment I mentioned that aspect of the story. He didn't speak; he continued to listen, but I could feel in the loosening grip of his hand and rapid breathing that he was experiencing a personal storm within his head. After several uncomfortable minutes of silence, he finally halted the movement of the walk and spun me to face him. I could make out the handsome features of his face even in the faint light of the half moon. I could smell his cologne and the sweetness of his breath as he pulled me close to him.

"We gonna get married, then," he announced, pulling me to his chest. I could feel his heart pounding against my face as he tightened his embrace. "I was already plannin' on askin' ya, but I thought it'd be best that we wait till I graduated. But this...this changes everything."

I didn't know what to say. His words spun and swirled around my ears but never quite entered my brain for compre-hension and processing. I remained silent as he continued to fill the air with endless ideas and plans for our future, including where we would live, the color wallpaper we would hang in the baby's room, which, he was certain was a boy; and even the fact that I didn't need to finish the rest of my schooling, that he would be the sole provider for the family. I could simply stay home and tend to our house and children. The sound of his words during that portion of the conversation both frightened and sickened me. Not that I didn't want to be his wife or a doting mother to our children, but I didn't like the sound nor idea of not being able to complete my education. I could admit that I was most certainly not the most studious pupil in Locust Ridge, but I did care about my learning, and I wanted to be able to finish high school along with the rest of the mountain kids and Sevierville townsfolk I had grown up with, even if I couldn't walk with them on graduation day. I had found peace and solace in finishing my schooling with Ms. Edna. Truth be told, my output had improved, both in written and test form. Ms. Edna was constantly remarking on the large strides I had made in such a short amount of time. I didn't want to just end all that.

"Kenneth," I finally interrupted him, "we have a lot to think about. First, I need to tell my momma. I'm not sure how she's gonna take all this. I don't wanna get too far ahead of ourselves until I take care of all the details in between."

"Right," Kenneth agreed, nodding his head and re-gripping my hand. We continued our walk around the edge of the farmland. We were nearing the barn, and the sound of Janice piddling and tinkering around within soon became obvious and noticeable. Naturally, we became quiet as we passed the old structure, the flickering light from Janice's sole torch glowing through the spaces between the wooden slats of the walls. She could even be heard muttering and mumbling to herself, but it didn't seem she was aware that we were there. After we had moved beyond the barn a good ways, Kenneth finally whispered, "I'm takin' ya with me tonight."

I pulled out of his grasp, the sting of his announcement cold and unsettling. "What...no," I whispered in return.

"Come on, Gen," he continued, raising his voice just above his previous tone. "I can't leave ya out here with these two."

Even in the dim moonlight, I could see his scowl of disapproval and disgust.

"I've heard all the stories about these two ladies, and none of it's good. In fact, it all just grosses me out. Let's go pack your things. I'll deal with the loud one."

"No, Kenneth," I heard myself say, my words shooting from my mouth before my brain even had the chance to think them. "I ain't leavin' here."

Kenneth remained quiet for a moment. Finally, he moved to embrace me.

"Okay," he whispered, pulling me to his chest. "Okay."

Not another word was spoken as we edged the front wooden fence of the property, slowly nearing the front porch of the cabin. I caught a brief glimpse of Ms. Edna peering from the screen door, but she was gone before I really had the chance to get a good look at her.

"I'll leave ya with this, Genevieve Delany," Kenneth said softly, brushing my hair back with his hand. "I'm in love with you, and now that you're havin' my baby, I swear I'll make ya my wife. I understand that this is all so fast and sudden, so I promise to move a bit slower, but I'm gonna do right, and that means providin' a home and life for you and our child."

I didn't say a word; I simply kept my eyes locked on his, a faint light from within the cabin causing his face to glow in a comforting orange hue.

I closed my eyes when he pulled me into his arms once again, this time smashing his lips over mine. Unlike before, his kiss felt cold and dominating, not warm and sensual like it had been in the past. The taste of his mouth nor the smell of his skin sent the excited, electrified urges into my lower extremities. Perhaps it was my current condition that prevented it, but there was certainly not an inkling of sexual yearning and desire like before. Just a few months ago, I could hardly keep my hands off him, much less not feel completely energized and overwhelmed by the touch of his lips or feeling of his mouth.

I watched as he waved from the driver's seat of his Daddy's giant Lincoln before accelerating down the gravel pathway toward the mountain road that would lead him back to Sevierville.

Ms. Edna didn't speak a word to me for the rest of the night, and I welcomed her silence. I completed my homework, enjoyed a cup of ginger tea, and carried myself to the lonely corner-side cot. Kenneth's words of promise and passion echoed around my brain as I fell into slumber, but the beating of my heart dulled any of his words' meaning and power. Aside from the grumbling in my belly, most likely from the tea, I fell asleep both empty and numb, unmoved and unexcited by any of the prospects of the seemingly endless proposals Kenneth had made.

⁎

MOMMA SHOWED UP ON Sunday evening. I was still swarming in my emotional spin regarding Kenneth and his marriage demand, let alone proposal, so I was certainly not prepared to face Momma. Not yet anyway, and not right now.

It didn't take her long to suspect something unusual in the air.

"What's the matter?" she finally asked after she had concluded her dinner. Ms. Edna and I barely touched our food.

"Well, Momma," I finally broke the silence, cueing Ms. Edna to leave the room, "there's somethin' I gotta tell ya."

Momma cried as I spoke, the truth falling from my lips nervous and heavy. To my surprise, she didn't get upset. She didn't yell, and she didn't strike me. Instead, she moved from her chair and to my side, pulling me toward her in a tight and consuming embrace. We stayed that way for quite a while, both crying, neither speaking a word.

Eventually, she moved back to her seat at the table, and the real discussion ensued.

"Does Kenneth know?" she finally asked, her eyes red and swollen from crying.

"Yes, he knows. He just found out on Friday."

"Dr. Reynolds told him?"

"No, I told him."

She stared at me curiously.

"How'd he know you was here?"

I hesitated, suddenly nervous to respond. There was no sense in playing dumb or acting clueless, so I told her the truth.

I could see her eyes change from sympathy to pain.

"There's somethin' we gotta discuss regardin' your Uncle John," she sighed. "Let's go for a walk."

Circling the farm property in nearly the exact same path Kenneth and I had taken just two nights prior, Momma and I moved along the backside of the yard toward the tree line.

In the distance, Janice's wall torch illuminated the interior of the barn.

"A big part of the reason I moved ya here is because I don't fully trust your uncle," she stated, keeping her eyes focused on the ground in front of her, the world around us darker and less visible than it had been when I was out here with Kenneth.

"Now, I want to be clear that he denies this, and I'm not insinuatin' anything," she continued, stopping in her tracks and turning me toward her.

"Your Uncle John had some issues when he was younger, issues that I'm afraid may still haunt him to this day."

I could feel her searching my face for an expression, but the shadows of the slow-moving clouds above prevented any celestial light from finding us. Unsure as to where she was going with this conversation, I simply stared back at her, waiting in breathless anticipation for the rest of what she was about to reveal.

"When we was kids, perhaps eleven and fifteen, he being fifteen, of course, somethin' happened."

I could feel her begin to shake slightly in the small space between us.

"Your uncle touched me, Gen," she said softly. "He touched me in a way a brother should never touch his baby sister."

Even in the darkness, I could sense her tears.

"So, I was afraid, with what ya say ya been experiencin' with your night terrors and all, that he may have had somethin' to do with it. I've always feared he might do somethin', but I had no other choice but to trust him with ya. And up until recently, I had no reason to worry that he had betrayed that trust. Like I said, he completely denies that he had anything to do with some of what ya say has happened, but I can't help but go there in my mind. I can't help but fear that that part of him is still there, just under the surface."

"No, Momma," I whispered. "I know Uncle John never touched me. Never."

"How can ya be so sure, hon? You was asleep most of the time."

I felt her hesitate before continuing.

"That was when he would do it to me, when I was sleepin'. But I would wake up. I'd pretend to stay asleep, but I could feel everything. I could..."

"Shh, Momma," I cooed, pulling her close to me. "That ain't what's happenin' here. I promise ya."

We continued to walk, rounding the south side of the barn, listening to Janice sing an old hymn to herself. The sound was striking and sweet, albeit a bit frightening as well as absolutely beautiful. Both Momma and I listened in silence until we were far enough away from the barn that we could no longer hear her.

Finally, Momma moved to conclude her visit.

"I can't take ya back to Gatlinburg," she said flatly, her face now glowing from the dim light from the barn. "I asked Mr. Barnes, begged even, but he simply can't allow me to keep you at the motel as a resident. Somethin' to do with his insurance or some nonsense. I'm not really sure, but the point is, he said no."

Her anger, disappointment, and worry were plain to see in the soft light between us. I could tell she felt defeated.

"I even threatened to quit. I still might. I can find another job there. I could get us a small apartment and—"

"Kenneth asked me to marry him," I announced, cutting her billowing rant short.

I could feel her staring at me intently, searching for an answer.

"And?" she whispered. "What did ya say?"

"Well," I began, choosing to ignore the fact that he more or less decided we were going to get married as opposed to truly asking or proposing. It didn't seem that Momma cared either way. She was more interested, if not excited, by the fact that he had mentioned it in the first place.

"This is wonderful, Gen!" she exclaimed, pulling me into her arms. I just stood still, allowing her to hug me but avoiding reciprocating the show of affection.

"Kenneth comes from good people, a good family. Not to mention his daddy is the town's only doctor. For sure you two will be taken care of while Kenneth gets the two of ya on your feet. When did he say he wants to do it? Has he spoken to his folks yet?"

I just shook my head, but Momma didn't seem to notice. She filled the next ten minutes with excited chatter about a quaint elopement ceremony, an event that would have to take place before my pregnancy really started to show. She even invited herself to stay with Kenneth and me, wherever that was to be, when it came time for me to deliver the baby.

I humored my mother. I did not respond to anything she said; I simply listened. She smiled and kissed my forehead before she left, her mood and demeanor a complete about-face from how it had been when she had first arrived.

Ms. Edna didn't ask me how it went. I think she heard enough from the front porch as Momma was saying goodbye. Once in bed, I pulled the quilt over my legs, stretching my toes until they edged the end of the cot. In the faint light, I stared at my belly, which was softly covered by the innocence of the single nightgown I had been wearing since the end of grade school. It was down to my ankles then; it now ended at the lower part of my thighs. In the darkness, I envisioned what was to come: a growing belly, a growing baby; an elopement, a new home; a marriage, a commitment; and an uncertainty and an ongoing fear of the still unknown. I fell asleep even more empty and hollow than I had the night after Kenneth had been here.

***

KENNETH SHOWED UP THE next day, just after breakfast, with a pickup truck and two buddies. The truck belonged to one of his friends, Ted Thompson, who was one of the two boys here now with Kenneth. Apparently, the three had cut school and were planning on leaving with me and my belongings in tow. I stormed toward the barn in anger; Kenneth followed, pleading for me to stop and listen to him.

"Gen, please!" he cried. "I just wanna do the right thing. My daddy agreed to let us stay on our own side of the house till we can get our own place. I've been talkin' to Ed Gentry down at the sawmill about lettin' me pick up a few shifts after school."

"What about football, Kenneth?" I reminded him, the sting of the cold morning air both exhilarating and painful. "Ya just gonna throw it all away? Ya just gonna let it all go to waste? The years of time and practice. What about college?"

Kenneth shook his head in disbelief. "College?" he scoffed. "Genevieve, do ya hear yourself? Ya do realize we gonna have a baby by the time I should be startin' my freshman year? It'll be hard enough to finish high school. I can just forget about college."

"And what does your daddy have to say about all this, Kenneth? He's fine with just lettin' his son throw all his dreams away just because he knocked up some girl from the hills?"

Kenneth stared at me for a moment before continuing. "Do ya really believe that I think of ya that way?" he asked, his face frowning. "I love ya, Gen. My daddy knows this. It don't matter what he thinks or wants. The fact of the matter is, I'm gonna do right by ya. I'm gonna provide for my wife and child. I'll make it through my senior year, and then I'll get somethin' full time. It's just the way it is, Gen. I ain't unhappy or upset. I guess I just wasn't meant to continue with football or go to college, is all."

I shook my head.

"No, Kenneth," I whispered, moving my eyes in the direction of the barn. I could see Janice peering suspiciously from one of the barn loft's glassless windows.

"I can't just let ya throw everything away. Why don't ya let me try to find a job near my momma in Gatlinburg? I could work at a diner or somethin'. You could come visit on weekends but continue with school and football. I'd be fine with that. My momma will help me."

Kenneth's frown turned to anger.

"Alright, I've heard just about all I'm gonna listen to!" he shouted. "I ain't listenin' to no more talk of ya movin' to Gatlinburg or me not bein' there and involved. It took the both of us to make this happen, and it's gonna take the both of us to see it through. We gettin' married, Gen, and I'm gonna make a life for us and our baby."

I continued to stare toward the barn. Janice was now tending to her woodchopping duties just out of sight. The sound of her ax as it pounded against the chopping stump echoed around the trees and between the various wood-framed buildings of the farm in a clapping thunder. Finally, I turned back to face Kenneth.

"I'm gonna finish school," I stated boldly. "Ms. Edna was kind enough to take me in and educate me. I wanna at least finish out what we started. I will come and live with you. I'll marry ya, even. But I ain't gonna quit my schoolin'."

Kenneth just looked at me for several seconds before nodding.

"Fine," he agreed. "I'll drive ya out here each mornin' before I go to school. We gonna have to leave at the crack of dawn's first light, but we'll manage."

I nodded, half smiling. I allowed him to hold me as he squeezed me tightly in the open field between the cabin and the barn. Despite his excitement, I just didn't share his enthusiasm for his plan for our future. I wanted to do the right thing. I knew the right thing to do was to marry him. I knew he could provide, and I knew, with his daddy's help, we would survive until Kenneth could get himself a good enough job to support us. Still, I hated the fact that he was going to sacrifice his original plans for the future, plans that involved getting a football scholarship to one of the state's, or nation's, top universities. I hated that he was going to settle for just working a local job straight out of high school, and I hated that the rest of his final school year was going to be burdened by the worry of work and the upcoming arrival of his first child. This was all too soon and sudden. This wasn't the way any of this was supposed to go.

I briefly explained to Ms. Edna what was happening as the three boys quickly loaded my belongings. I didn't have all that much, mostly just the duffel bags and trash bags full of clothing and shoes Momma and I had brought a month or so prior. I promised Ms. Edna I would see her in the morning, apologized for the sudden and unexpected chaos, kissed her cheek, and joined Kenneth and the boys on the front bench seat of the truck. Kenneth held my hand as Ted floored the accelerator of the old pickup. Jim Anderson, the third boy, was holding on tightly in the bag-filled truck bed behind us. I watched as Ms. Edna disappeared in the rearview mirror as Ted swerved the truck from the end of the gravel pathway and onto the country road that would lead us to town. My stomach began to ache and churn as we journeyed further toward Sevierville. Although I had agreed to go along with the majority of Kenneth's plans, I couldn't help but feel I had made the wrong choice.

***

KENNETH'S HOME, WHERE HE had lived since he was a young boy, was a large two-story house at the end of one of the nicest streets in Sevierville. Sevierville wasn't a wealthy town, but it did have its quaint, all-American, picturesque rows of houses, much the same as many country towns around the state. The houses here, and especially Kenneth's, were worlds away from the cabins and small wood-framed houses I was familiar with back in Locust Ridge.

The front door opened to a grand staircase. Framed paintings and books lined the walls and nearby shelves. A crystal chandelier hung above, its countless teardrop-like pieces causing a rainbow effect on the floor near the door. I followed Kenneth up the stairs to his room. He pointed out the area of the house that was to be ours. His parents, Dr. Reynolds and his mother, June Reynolds, a woman I had only met once before, agreed to allow us our own portion of the house, but only after we were married. Apparently, according to Kenneth, we were to wed in less than a month.

Dr. Reynolds was at work at his office, but Mrs. Reynolds stalked around the staircase and corridors Kenneth and the two boys moved between while unloading my things. Eventually, once Ted and Jim had left, Kenneth, Mrs. Reynolds, and I all sat down for lunch. Mrs. Reynolds served us. There were no fancy housemaids, servants, or butlers as I had expected. The house was certainly grand and impressive, but nowhere near the palace I had imagined it to be.

Kenneth dominated the lunch conversation, while Mrs. Reynolds and I exchanged curious looks and glances whenever the other wasn't looking. She had yet to say much more to me than a casual and semi-warm hello. Her assuming and awkward glances had me feeling more than uncomfortable, much in the same way her husband, Dr. Reynolds, had peered at me cautiously and suspiciously the day he came to perform the checkup. Mrs. Reynolds darted her eyes in my direction only to take in brief stares. She never once locked eyes with me nor smiled. In fact, I hadn't seen her smile once since we had arrived. Kenneth didn't seem to notice nor care. He continued to babble on about various details of schoolboy pranks, football nonsense, and the afterparty plans he and his friends had for their upcoming senior prom. A slight ache filled my core as I listened to him detail the school's prom plans. Thanks to Mr. and Mrs. Watson, Emily's parents, Sevierville High enjoyed a lavish and decorative prom each year. A piece of me sank as I realized I wasn't going to be able to experience my own senior prom when the time came, nor was I going to be allowed to attend Kenneth's as his date.

With lunch through, Kenneth led the way back upstairs, his room a hodgepodge of football paraphernalia, trophies, textbooks, and all my clothing. I started to maneuver my way through the mess toward the piles of bags in the corner, my only possessions in the chaos, but was interrupted by Kenneth.

"Momma went to lie down," he whispered, the touch of his breath causing my skin to prickle and tingle. "I think we should fool around a bit."

"No," I whispered, returning my focus to the bags. "I wanna get settled in. Plus, I'm not feelin' all that well today. My stomach hurts."

Kenneth remained in place behind me, his breathing signaling his disappointment and annoyance. Eventually, he moved toward the corner of the room and began tossing the various piles of his littered clothing into a single basket. We didn't speak for the rest of the afternoon. He left me to lie down about an hour later. I watched the shadows dancing on the ceiling as I attempted to fall asleep, my brain spinning from all the sudden newness and unexpected change. I didn't wake up until Dr. Reynolds came home.

***

THE FIRST THREE DAYS of living with the Reynoldses was uncomfortable, to say the least. Dr. Reynolds continued to glare and peer at me curiously, much in the same way as when he had made the house call to Ms. Edna's, and Mrs. Reynolds hardly spoke more than a handful of general sentences to me, despite my best effort to converse with her. Thankfully, much of my day was spent with Ms. Edna; Kenneth and I would leave the house before dawn, and by the time he left school and picked me up in the late afternoon, it was nearly dark once we returned to his parents' house.

It was Thursday evening of the first week there that Dr. Reynolds and I found ourselves alone in the house. Mrs. Reynolds was attending a meeting with her church's ladies' prayer group, and Kenneth was at football practice. I was in the kitchen, clearing the dinner dishes, when Dr. Reynolds approached me from behind.

"I didn't realize my son was the father of your baby," he stated plainly, standing in the middle of the kitchen. "You can imagine my surprise when he told me. I had no idea the two of you were even seein' each other."

"Yes," I replied nervously from the massive porcelain sink. "Not for very long though. It's still new."

"I see," Dr. Reynolds commented, the sound of his voice detailing his disapproval. "Well, listen, I'm not gonna beat around the bush. My wife and I are not thrilled with all this. It isn't personal toward ya, Genevieve. We just wish Kenneth had finished school and had a chance to attend a university before settlin' down with a wife and child."

"I agree, Dr. Reynolds," I said, keeping my attention in the direction of the sink. "I told Kenneth I would be fine movin' to Gatlinburg with my momma, workin' to help support the baby. Kenneth could come see us on weekends, finish school, and even go to college. I wanted that for him. I didn't insist that we get married and move in with you. I wanted what was best for everyone. Kenneth didn't plan this, nor did I. It just happened."

Seemingly stunned by my honest and lengthy response, I could feel the doctor inch closer to me.

"Is that so?" he asked quietly, perhaps more to himself than to me. "Thank ya for your frankness. It is appreciated. Perhaps, in time, circumstances will allow for Kenneth to attend school after all."

I wasn't quite sure what he meant by that, but I turned around to face him, smiling. He cracked a half smile in return, nodded his head, and darted his eyes away as quickly as possible. For whatever reason, Dr. Reynolds always seemed to have an issue with keeping eye contact with me. His wife would often stare and glare, mostly when she thought I couldn't see her, but Dr. Reynolds, a doctor whose profession had him talking face-to-face with various patients on a daily basis, appeared shy, awkward, and uncomfortable around me. It was like my very presence triggered some sort of insecurity within him. It was both odd and unnerving.

He turned and left the kitchen. The entire brief encounter left me uneasy for the rest of the night. I fell asleep in Kenneth's arms. All but the first night, we made love, although it was far more obligatory for me than it was enjoyable. I did love Kenneth, and I was still attracted to him, but there was something missing. Something different. It had changed. Perhaps it was because now there was a reality to our connection; an expectation placed on the bond by the definition and restraints of society. I felt far more excited and aroused by the mystery of Kenneth than the actual young man himself. Fantasy: the bane in our acceptance of what is. I fell asleep still unnerved by Kenneth's father.

***

"SO, HOW'RE THINGS BACK at home?" Ms. Edna asked as we concluded another day of homeschooling. "Settlin' in okay?"

I smiled and shrugged.

"It's fine, I guess."

"You guess?" Ms. Edna peeked at me over her spectacles. "What's the matter, dear?"

Smirking, I shook my head. "Nothin'," I lied. "I think I just miss Uncle John, is all. I haven't seen him in so long."

Ms. Edna nodded but didn't speak a word. There wasn't much she could say anyhow. The last time I had seen my uncle, Ms. Edna had chased him from the property with a shotgun. Of course, I was disturbed by what Momma had revealed to me about him, but despite the heartbreaking details, I still did not feel that my uncle played any part in the goings-on of my night terrors. Thankfully, I hadn't had an episode in months. Ever since I moved to Ms. Edna's, and then to Kenneth's, not a single night event occurred. Looking at it from that perspective, it certainly did place a mountain of suspicion over Uncle John. Still, I loved him, and I most certainly did miss him. I could only hope he was doing okay out there by himself, despite the circumstances of his past, and aside from his apparent addiction. Perhaps I was just blissfully ignorant, but either way, I couldn't help how I felt about him.

Kenneth was cold during the car ride home. I attempted to initiate some small talk with him, but he shut everything down before it could even get started. Finally, he broke his silence and flooded the car with his most current life frustration.

"Daddy won't let me take the job at the mill," he huffed. "Here Ed Gentry went outta his way to get me an after-school position, and my own fuckin' dad forbids it."

He turned his head toward me, waiting for my eyes to meet his. "We gonna haveta move out."

I stared back at him, my expression blank.

"I'm just gonna quit school, take the sawmill job full time. We could stay in Ted Thompson's barn while I save the money to get us a place."

"No," I shook my head. "Ya haveta finish school, Kenneth. I won't allow ya to—"

"Allow me?" he scoffed. "Ya gonna be my wife soon, Genevieve. Ya won't have very much say so over the decisions I make. In fact, ya won't have much of a say at all. I'll be the man of the house."

"You mean barn," I quipped, snapping my head away from him.

"Don't get smart, Gen," he mumbled.

We pulled into the driveway, where Dr. Reynolds was waiting.

"Ya gonna have to find another way to take her out there," he announced the moment Kenneth and I exited the car and began the trek up the long brick-paved pathway to the front of the house.

"What?" Kenneth replied, dropping his leather knapsack to the ground, several hardcover textbooks sliding out onto the brick.

"I'm sellin' the Continental. We don't need it."

Kenneth just stared at his father, a storm of extreme emotions clearly brewing behind his eyes.

"What do ya mean *we don't need it*?" he fired back, appearing to try to control his rage. "I need it to get to school, and I need it to take her out for her schoolin'. We need this car, Dad."

"You can take the damn bus, and it ain't our fault she was expelled. Perhaps her hillbilly ass shoulda thought about the consequences before placin' her hands on the town's most influential family's daughter. Her mistakes are not ours to suffer."

Kenneth spun toward the front of the Continental, punching one of the headlights. It didn't break, causing him to pull his fist back in pain.

"Keep it up, Kenneth," his father shouted from the upper part of the driveway. "I'll take the keys tonight if ya don't watch it."

I walked toward Kenneth, but not before Dr. Reynolds met my eyes with a disapproving smirk. It was the first time he kept eye contact with me for more than a few seconds.

"We haveta get outta here this week," Kenneth mumbled once I made it to his side. "I'm gonna call Ted tonight."

I didn't resist nor respond. I simply sighed and waited for Kenneth to gather his books and knapsack, and followed him inside.

I listened as Kenneth confirmed the details of moving into Ted Thompson's family barn with Ted on the telephone. We were to move in on the weekend, just three days from now. I didn't say a word as Kenneth demanded that we start packing our things. Once again, I shoved my entire life into a few duffel bags and some tattered trash bags. By the end of the week, I would be living in a barn.

***

DR. REYNOLDS CONFISCATED KENNETH'S car keys on Friday morning. Ted Thompson took me out to Ms. Edna's while Kenneth arranged the rest of our belongings. Both Kenneth and Ted arrived that afternoon in Ted's pickup. I didn't tell Ms. Edna what was happening; I didn't want to worry her. Instead, I jumped inside the cab and listened to the two boys chat excitedly about how great it was going to be living so close to each other. I only smiled and nodded when asked a question, but I never contributed to the unrelatable babble between the two high-school football buddies. We were to stay one final night at Kenneth's parent's place, arriving to the barn first thing Saturday morning.

Dinner that evening was so incredibly uncomfortable that you could practically cut the tension with just your bare finger. Mrs. Reynolds never spoke a word, but Kenneth and his father exchanged cutting remarks and disapproving statements throughout the thirty-minute meal.

"This is the biggest mistake of your life, son," Dr. Reynolds stated, shoveling a spoonful of mashed potatoes into his mouth.

"Ya gave me no choice, Dad," Kenneth remarked.

"Ya gave yourself no choice!" the doctor shouted, spitting half-chewed mashed potatoes all over the table. Quietly, I slid one the of discarded bits from the corner of my plate with the subtlety of my pinky.

I didn't flinch nor react when Dr. Reynolds repeatedly insulted me from the head of the table. It was clear I wasn't good enough for his son. According to him, I was easy, and it was obvious that he despised me more than any other human being in his life. I accepted this and simply kept my mouth shut. Kenneth did little to defend me whenever his father would refer to me by some form of a derogatory name or term. Instead, he kept the focus of his counterattacks on his father personally.

Still, we went to bed that night defeated. The car was to be sold, we were no longer welcome in the home if Kenneth quit school, and both parents would now not be attending our wedding ceremony, whenever that was to be.

I fell asleep that night exhausted and ashamed. How did I manage to get myself into all this? Perhaps all the old-timey mountain preachers were right: sins of the flesh really were the playground for the devil.

***

THAT NIGHT, I AWOKE to excruciating pain. I sat up, soaked in tears and sweat. Something had happened. I could feel it. My entire body felt altered, invaded. I had no memory of a night terror; I was still in bed beside Kenneth, but I knew without a shadow of any doubt that something was wrong.

My head was heavy and weighted; my lower abdomen was sore. There was an odd numb sensation coming from my lower regions. From my navel down to my toes, everything buzzed and tingled, almost as though my entire lower body had fallen asleep. I attempted to coax myself back into slumber but remained in a painful state of sheer fear for the rest of the night. About an hour and a half later, I could see the sun starting to peek through the blinds. It was dawn. I managed to shake Kenneth awake, but he too was experiencing the same heavy-headedness and groggy mentality.

"God, I feel like shit," he complained, slowly lifting his body from the bed. "I feel like I got hammered last night, but I didn't have anything to drink but some cola."

I didn't mention my pain; it had nearly subsided anyhow. Instead, I joined him in dressing and maneuvering the packed clothing and other various supplies. Kenneth had managed to sneak some canned goods from the kitchen pantry. This was a relief. I had wondered how or what we were going to eat back there in the rustic barn behind the Thompson household. Were they going to feed us scraps alongside their pen of pigs, or would we be given some handfuls of chicken feed each morning?

Ted arrived a little after seven. He assisted in loading the truck bed with Kenneth's and my things, and joined us in the front cab. Ted let Kenneth drive. Apparently, he was going to be using the truck to get back and forth from work after he dropped Ted and me off at our designated places of learning. Ted, of course, still attended Sevierville High, whereas I was allotted a farm out in the back hills of Locust Ridge, and Kenneth was now no longer in school altogether. Ted was a good friend to Kenneth, but I wasn't sure if his friendship was a benefit or a further hindrance at this point.

We moved our things into the backside of the Thompson family barn. It was a large structure, perhaps the same size as the barn on Janice and Ms. Edna's property, but theirs, the Thompson's, was in far worse condition.

Thankfully, there were no animals in the barn, only tractors, trucks, and other various farm equipment. The backside of the building had been cleared out, recently too. The floor was freshly swept of hay and dirt debris, exposing an uneven, cracked, and holey wooden floor. I got a splinter in no less than ten minutes of removing my shoes.

Kenneth and I worked the rest of the day making the most of our new home. Ted provided us an old mattress, a twin-size. It had been his; he was now going to share a full-size with his older brother, Marcus. I could only imagine how both Kenneth and I were going to fit on a twin-sized mattress. Back at his parent's house, we enjoyed the luxury and comfort of a queen-sized, but here in the barn, our dirty and drafty new home, a twin-sized mattress was the new definition of luxury. It sure as hell beat sleeping on a quilt-covered pile of hay, the original bed solution proposed by Kenneth.

The Thompson family invited us in for dinner, an occurrence that Ms. Thompson, a single mother of four children, made clear could not become a regularity. She didn't say it with any sort of discord; she was simply being realistic with us. She could barely afford to feed the mouths she had under her roof as it was, never mind two nearly grown adults who now occupied the back corner of her barn.

Kenneth wanted to make love that night, but I resisted him. The numbness of my lower body had long faded, leaving me sore and irritated. The last thing I wanted was for something to be stuck inside me, much less aggressively thrusting for any length of time. Instead, I could hear Kenneth masturbating in the dark. He wasn't trying to be secretive about it, for he turned over and spilled himself all over the front of my nightgown as he climaxed. I waited until he fell asleep before removing the garment. Tossing it in the front corner of the barn, near the door, I planned to discard of it in the morning, feeling as though it had now been sullied and violated. I returned to the mattress in just my bra and panties. This was fine since the barn only grew hotter as the night progressed. Several times I awoke in a drenched sweat, the feeling of Kenneth's nighttime erection poking at my back. God, to be a male and remain so horny, even while sleeping, must be so damn bothersome.

Kenneth was awake before me, busy heating some eggs on a borrowed skillet over a small fire. I watched in silence at the scene before me. Here was a boy I had known for many years but had only recently gotten to know better, not to mention become intimate with, and now I was watching him prepare two eggs he had most likely swiped from a nearby chicken coop over a tiny flame ignited on a pathetic scrap heap of old rags, trash, and dried hay. Even though I grew up in a basic hand-to-mouth existence, I never once had to prepare food by a flame on the floor, let alone steal my breakfast from some nearby farm's chicken house.

I joined Kenneth on the floor for breakfast. He was excited by his ability to provide, and I merely obliged him by consuming the solo egg and refraining from speaking. It was when I stood to my feet that Kenneth's expression morphed from a smile to one of complete panic.

"You're bleeding!" he said breathlessly, pointing between my legs.

I looked down at my white cotton panties. Indeed, there was a large crimson stain directly over my vagina. I felt myself fall to my knees in a mixture of terror and disbelief.

Before I knew it, Kenneth had me covered in the bed quilt, carrying me in his arms toward the borrowed pickup truck.

Within twenty minutes, we were pulling into his parents' driveway.

Dr. and Mrs. Reynolds were just piling into Dr. Reynolds's Cadillac, yellow in color, far newer than the bright-green Lincoln Continental Kenneth had been using, the one that was now deemed for sale. They were headed to church, until we stopped them.

"Daddy!" Kenneth screamed, his voice shrill and high. The sound alone was enough to frighten me. "Ya gotta look at Gen. She's bleedin'!"

Kenneth snatched me from the passenger side of the truck, lifted me into his arms, and scrambled for the front door of his childhood home. I could see both Mr. and Mrs. Reynolds following us inside. Mrs. Reynolds darted her head in the direction of the street, obviously fearful that some nosey neighbor might overhear and witness the embarrassing commotion.

Kenneth laid me on the floor of the foyer.

"Don't let her bleed on my rug," Mrs. Reynolds declared, clutching her pearls and black leather purse.

Dr. Reynolds went to fetch his medical bag. Upon returning, he performed a fast and hasty examination before concluding that I had miscarried. I swore I heard Mrs. Reynolds mutter, "Thank the Lord," under her breath, but I couldn't be certain.

Kenneth started crying before I did. I looked on from the floor as he fell into his father's arms in a heaping fit of sobbing. Mrs. Reynolds simply left the room.

***

KENNETH BARELY SPOKE TO me for the next few days. The reality of my miscarriage had yet to fully set in for me, whereas Kenneth was experiencing a grieving process. It was both odd and touching to see him so affected by this. I had only been pregnant a few weeks, yet Kenneth lamented around as if his best friend had died.

Finally, on the morning of the fourth day after the bleeding had begun, I awoke to the sound of my own sobbing. I couldn't believe it. One moment I was fine: pregnant, tired, but healthy. The next, I had lost everything. I still couldn't shake the idea that there was something more to all this. Why had I awakened that night in pain? The feeling was exactly the same as the majority of my night terrors: the heavy-headedness, the confusion and lower-body pain. Was it possible that something or someone had directly affected or even initiated the miscarriage? Perhaps it was something I had eaten? Maybe it was all the near-nightly sex? I had awoken on my stomach a few times; perhaps I had squashed the baby? Every possible scenario of guilt-stricken accusation filled and swarmed my head for the entirety of the day. I didn't say a word to anyone until halfway through the school day with Ms. Edna.

She held me as I wept after I had concluded the tale of my current existence. She petted and kissed my hair, laying her head on top of mine. I couldn't speak for a least an hour. Ms. Edna wrapped me in a blanket and had me sit near the fireplace. A small ember still burned beneath the pile of blackened ashes.

I enjoyed a cup of ginger tea before Kenneth arrived in Ted's truck to fetch me. Something was immediately different the very second I closed the truck door.

"Are you okay?" I finally asked as we weaved the country roads toward Sevierville. "You're awfully quiet."

"I'm fine," Kenneth retorted, keeping his eyes locked out the windshield.

I could hear him huffing and sighing loudly before he finally found the courage to speak the words he had been dying to say.

"I can't help but feel this is your fault," he stated, not allowing his eyes to stray from in front of him.

"How can ya say that?" I whispered, instant tears flooding my face.

"I don't know," he muttered. "I mean, you're a young girl. Healthy. I just don't understand how ya could just suddenly miscarry like that. No warnin'. Nothin'."

"That's how it happens, Kenneth," I spat through a tearful gaze. "Ya don't think I haven't blamed myself already?"

"So you're sayin' this is your fault, then?" he shouted, finally turning his face toward me. "What did ya do, Genevieve?"

I was in a state of shock. I couldn't believe Kenneth was somehow trying to blame me for the miscarriage.

"Did ya take somethin'? Drink somethin'? Did one of those pussy-eatin' dykes do somethin' to ya?"

"No!" I screamed, my voice hollow from crying, my eyes blurry and stained from the water.

"I can't handle this, Gen," Kenneth continued, tears now staining his own face. "I just can't be around this."

"What are ya sayin'?" I asked in a half whisper.

"I'm sayin'..."

He turned his head back in the direction of the windshield, visibly preparing himself for what he was about to say next.

"I'm sayin' I think we should spend some time apart, is all. I think I'm gonna move back in with Momma and Daddy. Maybe you can stay with your uncle for a while."

I couldn't believe the words that were coming out of Kenneth's mouth. He was abandoning me. He was through. Our loss was now only his.

I didn't say a word as he turned the truck in the direction of Uncle John's cabin. Before I knew it, we were pulling up to the edge of the property, Uncle John's overgrown fields visible in the distance. It appeared he hadn't plowed in weeks, months even. The height of the weeds and grass made it difficult to make out the location of the cabin. If it weren't for the aluminum vents that dotted the sides of the roof, I would have missed it completely.

"I'll come back for ya in a week or so," Kenneth announced, tossing the truck in park.

"I get no say in this whatsoever?" I begged, my voice weak and wavering. "I miscarry, and you just toss me away? I thought we was gonna get married? I thought you was gonna provide for us?"

"Yeah, for *us*. The baby."

I could see more tears welling in his eyes.

"But that's gone now, Gen. I need time to heal. I need to be with my folks."

I shook my head but didn't utter another sound. I hadn't noticed, but all my things were piled in the back of the truck. I stared in a tear-heavy silence as Kenneth unloaded my belongings, got back behind the wheel, and sped away, leaving me standing curbside at the edge of my uncle's side of our vast family property. I had been tossed away. Deserted. Never in my entire life had I felt so incredibly sick, both physically and psychologically.

***

UNCLE JOHN DIDN'T ASK many questions as he helped me drag the bags of my possessions from the side of the road. He seemed to understand my need for silence. I didn't want to talk about what had just occurred. I didn't even want him to mention Kenneth's name. I didn't eat when he served dinner. I couldn't, even if I had tried. I stayed in Uncle John's bed, the pain in my stomach more emotional than physical. I cried until my tear ducts hurt. I cried until the water of my body had long been depleted.

Uncle John kept his distance. He brought me a few glasses of water, which I did consume, and left me to my tears. He was nowhere to be seen the next morning, but I also did not put much effort into finding him. Stumbling, I made my way from the cabin door toward the outhouse, falling to my knees halfway in a fit of vomiting and dry heaving. Uncle John appeared at my side.

He waited outside the outhouse as I succumbed to diarrhea. I wasn't sure if the movement was from nerves or something viral. I didn't care. I wanted to die. Everything I had come to know and accept as my life had been snatched away in a matter of a day or so. I had lost my baby, and now, I had lost Kenneth. I had no desire to go on.

Uncle John helped me from the outhouse and back into bed. I remained there the rest of the day, cycling in and out of consciousness and bouts of extensive sobbing. Before I knew it, it was dark again, and Uncle John was once more offering me dinner. This time, though, he didn't take no for an answer.

I found myself propped at the table, Uncle John's bed quilt still surrounding my shoulders, his pillow smashed between my back and the back of the chair.

"Ya have to eat, hon," Uncle John commanded from his side of the small kitchen table. "It's just broth, but ya need somethin' in your stomach."

"I can't," I whispered, my face heavy and raw from constant crying. "I'll just toss it up."

"No ya won't," Uncle John replied, nodding to the soup. "Eat, Gen. Don't make me force ya."

I could feel him watching as I methodically placed the old spoon in my mouth, returning it to the soup bowl for more liquid, and then repeating the motion. I did this at last twenty times before I finally gave up. Apparently, it was deemed enough by Uncle John, and I was allowed to return to the bed. Along the way, I spotted a syringe tucked beneath some old newspaper. I opted not to say anything. I didn't have the strength. Instead, I fell onto the bed, snuggled into the oversized handsewn quilt, and fell asleep from both physical and mental exhaustion. When I awoke again, Uncle John was asleep on the sofa, the full moon beaming in through the bedside window. In the dark, I stared at the moon, its glow eventually causing my eyes to ache. In the silence of the stillness, I cursed God for all he had allowed to transpire. He had taken my baby before she could be born; he had taken my promised security and future. Now, here I was, alone with Uncle John, a man who as a teenager had inappropriately touched his kid sister and who was now enslaved to a morphine addiction. I craved to see my momma, imagining her comforting arms wrapped tightly around me as I cried out the ongoing river of internal pain. I thought I saw a star move as I finally faded into a session of sleep, its movement fast and controlled near the side of the massive full moon.

***

UNCLE JOHN LET ME be for most of the next three or four days. I had lost count of the days; I had lost all sense of time. The sun would rise and set beyond the windows of the house; I was back at home, but between minor attempts at eating and visiting the bathroom, I didn't venture very far from my bed. Uncle John would check in on me at least twice a day. He would force me to eat some toast in the morning, ensured I had enough water to last the day, and would then reappear later in the evening to encourage me to eat something for dinner. Slowly, I began to feel a bit better, both physically and emotionally, and I asked Uncle John if he would take me back to Ms. Edna's. Hesitantly, he agreed. I could tell he didn't want me to go. He knew returning me there meant he wasn't going to see me much, but he could tell it was not only what I wanted, but also what I needed, especially now.

Without Momma around more, I needed a female guidance and support system. I needed someone who could love and nurture me in the ways Uncle John couldn't, even though he tried. As much as my uncle loved and worked to protect me, he simply could not give me what a woman could. Worn, used, and discarded by a man, I needed a female presence during my time of healing, not another male.

"How ya doin', hon?" Ms. Edna asked, helping me from Uncle John's truck and onto the gravel driveway. "I've been so very worried."

She held me close, nodding at Uncle John, who nodded in return, shifted the truck into gear, and drove slowly back toward the road.

Ms. Edna and I remained in front of the cabin for a while, just holding each other, allowing the breeze of the early morning mountain air to cool and surround us. Finally, after what must have been more than ten minutes, Ms. Edna pulled me inside, and we began our lessons as though no time had transpired since the last time we were together. I made it clear that I wasn't yet able to discuss what had happened. I didn't have to say too much. Ms. Edna could just tell by my overall silence and demeanor. Around lunchtime, Janice entered the cabin.

"What's the matter?" she asked the moment her eyes met mine. "Why ya so sad?"

I started to cry, without warning or any form of control; I just wept, the tears weighing my head down to the table.

"Dammit, Janice," I heard Ms. Edna say as she rushed to my side. "Just leave us be. I'll call ya when it's time to eat."

About an hour later, the three of us sat silently at the kitchen table. Ms. Edna had fixed us some ham sandwiches, the meat provided by one of my favorite pigs, Franklin. Ms. Edna had warned me never to name the livestock and to try my hardest not to become attached to them. Still, I couldn't help it. Franklin was special. He'd always rush to my side the moment I entered his pen and would trail behind me as I performed my chore of refilling the troughs and changing out the water bowls. Although I knew this time would eventually come, it affected me now far more intensely than perhaps it would have had I not just recently experienced so much personal trauma. I excused myself to the outhouse and remained there for the rest of the lunchtime.

Later that evening, as I sat alone on the front porch swing, my eyes fixed on the pot of sprouted wheat seeds, Janice approached and sat down beside me.

"Is your baby doin' okay?" she asked, almost childlike.

"No, Janice," I whispered, surprised that my answer didn't unleash another swell of tears. Perhaps I had already depleted my body's resources for tears. Perhaps there wasn't another ounce of water left inside my body to provide yet another endless stream down my face. Or perhaps I was slowly becoming numb to my ongoing and relentless pain.

"What's the matter?" she continued, rolling her dirt-plastered hands around each other.

"I lost it," I confirmed, keeping my eyes on the small ceramic pot on the floor. "My baby's gone."

"I knew it," I heard Janice whisper. "They took it."

I closed my eyes and sighed, in no mood to hear Janice's wild tales of the mysterious strangers in the woods nor their interest in me, especially not some plot to kidnap my unborn child.

"No, Janice," I said, turning my head in her direction. "I had a miscarriage."

Janice didn't return my gaze. She kept her eyes fixed on the nervous fumbling of her hands.

Finally, the old woman dropped one of her work-worn, withered hands over mine.

"I'm sorry, child," she said softly. "I'm truly sorry."

She didn't wait for a reply. She lifted herself from the old porch swing and limped back toward the barn. I watched her disappear out of sight, her gentle concern and kindness lingering where she had just touched my hand.

***

"SHH," JANICE WHISPERED, PLACING a hand over my mouth.

I had been asleep on my cot, the darkness of the cabin surrounding us in a featureless void. I could make out Janice's face, which was panicked yet focused, from the faint light that trickled in from the nearby living room window.

"They here," she continued, lowering her eyes to mine. "Don't speak. They know you here. I saw one of 'em headin' this way, so I came through the back door. I have my gun."

My heart began to race. What the hell was going on? Where was Ms. Edna? Should I scream and wake her? Janice was obviously having another one of her episodes. Should I be afraid? Would she hurt me, unintentionally or otherwise? I decided to take my chances by sitting up on the cot.

"Look," Janice pointed toward the large living room window. Through the sheer white of the handsewn lace curtains, I saw it: a figure. It stood in the center of the window, completely motionless, but it was there. In the distance between the cot and the curtains, you could feel the presence; you could feel it watching you.

"What is it, Janice?" I whispered, pushing myself into her body. She stood next to me, her knee on the lower end of the cot. In her left hand was her shotgun. She moved her right arm from around my shoulder and toward the weapon. In the blackness, I could hear her cock the gun.

"What's goin' on out here?" Ms. Edna's voice boomed across the room. I returned my eyes to the window. The figure was gone.

"Dammit, Edna," Janice exclaimed. "He got away!"

Janice bolted from the cot and toward the kitchen. The back screen door could be heard opening and slamming shut.

Ms. Edna and I just stared at each other.

"I saw it, Ms. Edna," I admitted. "There was somethin' standin' at the window. I saw it with my own eyes."

"Oh, bologna, the both of ya," Ms. Edna huffed, snatching at the end of her nightgown and moving into the kitchen. "Ya didn't see anything but what Janice wanted ya to see. It was dark. The mind and our eyes love to play tricks. There wasn't nothin' there."

"No, but, Ms. Edna, really. I did see it. I could feel it, too. I could feel whatever it was just starin' back at me. It gave me such a chill..."

When I finally moved into the kitchen, Ms. Edna was busy preparing tea. I sat at my usual chair at the kitchen table, suddenly nervous and frightened. I suppose Ms. Edna could sense it or see the emotion written on my face, for she attempted to somehow calm my nerves with a story to tag along with her offering of cinnamon tea.

"I did see somethin' myself once," she admitted, stirring her tea with an old spoon. "It was years back. At least twenty or more now, but I remember it. Janice and I had just bought a pair of goats. We named 'em Marty and Molly. One night, around Christmas, we heard the goats cryin' out somethin' awful. The sound still haunts me to this day. Janice and I ran out to the barn, where their pen was. We saw a little man, short, gray pale skin. He was kneeling over Molly, some kinda rod in his hand. Marty was runnin' around kickin' and screamin', but Molly was down on the floor, completely out of it. The thing took one fast glance at us and then vanished. We didn't see where he went or how he even managed to make it outta the barn without us noticin'. I mean, there is only one way in and out of that place. But he was gone. I still remember it though. The eyes. He had these massive eyes. Wide and black like a screech owl's. I could feel him lookin' into me, even in just that fast glance. It was like...I don't know. It was like I could hear his voice or somethin', but only in my head."

I stared at Ms. Edna in complete and utter disbelief. What was she saying? She actually saw one of the little men crazy

Janice ranted about? I suddenly became afraid for my safety. Perhaps these two old ladies really were as batty and insane as everyone made them out to be. I swallowed nervously, tightly clutching the ceramic mug in my hands.

"So I did see somethin," she continued, lowering her mug onto the table. "But it was only that one time. It never happened again. I ain't never seen anything like it in decades, and I refuse to believe anything is happenin' now. Janice, well, her mind don't work like it used to. She flashes back to things. She remembers everything backwards. She's often stuck on some conundrum that happened twenty or thirty years ago. The other day she was in here talkin' to me as if I were her momma. She ain't right, so we can't trust that what she says she is seein' is really even there...even if I did indeed see somethin' myself once."

"What happened to Molly?" I finally asked, unsure if I should even be encouraging this conversation.

Ms. Edna sighed, hesitating. Nervously, she returned her mug to her lips, sipping the steaming contents slowly and carefully. It was clear that she was taking the moment to choose her words cautiously and purposefully.

"She'd been pregnant," she started, lowering her mug back to the table. "She was just a few months along. After that night though..." Ms. Edna moved her eyes toward the back door. "Well...after that night, she wasn't pregnant anymore."

I could feel my pulse accelerate, beads of sweat forming over my brow.

"Now, don't go thinkin' this has anything to do with what has recently happened to you, darlin'. This was all a very long time ago, and it all means nothin', it's just—"

I vomited all over the table. Ms. Edna stared in a stunned silence for a moment before lifting from her chair to fetch a dishtowel. I didn't move from my chair as she quickly and diligently wiped my face, neck, and the table top.

Neither of us spoke another word as she guided me back into the living room and secured me beneath the quilts that lay across the cot.

I stared at the living room window for at least an hour before falling asleep. I didn't know what to think or what to believe. The very thought of any of it just made me sick to my stomach. Eventually, mental and physical exhaustion dominated, and I succumbed to slumber. In my dreams, I saw it: the little man, his pale gray skin, his dark and wide eyes, glaring, staring, somehow listening to the sound of my thoughts.

***

THERE WAS NO MORE talk of the incident, little gray men, Marty or Molly, or even my miscarriage. Janice, per usual, tended to her laborious farm chores and duties, and Ms. Edna and I continued our homeschooling. Momma telephoned on Friday night, and I tearfully told her of the entire ordeal. My voice wavered as I spoke of my brief time living with the Reynoldses. My tears streamed as I told her about the miscarriage, and I began to sob when I recounted the day Kenneth dropped me off at Uncle John's. Momma listened quietly, only whispering her words of pain and regret. I could hear her sobbing on the other end of the phone line. She promised to visit within the next week. Mr. Barnes had taken ill, and Momma was now running the motel as its full-time manager. She barely had any time off, not enough to sneak off to Locust Ridge, some half hour or more away. I said goodbye to Momma and hung up the phone. I didn't speak to anyone for the rest of the night.

Ms. Edna and I awoke to the sound of shouting. It was Saturday morning, early; the sun had just begun to peek out over the nearby mountaintops. Ms. Edna opened the front door, revealing Kenneth, his hair disheveled, his clothes torn and stained. His face was smeared in what appeared to be both dried blood and dirt.

"What the devil?" Ms. Edna whispered, attempting to close the door.

"Gen!" Kenneth shouted, snatching open the screen door and pushing past Ms. Edna.

"Gen, baby." He started to cry, falling to his knees before me. "I'm so sorry, baby."

I just looked down at him while he sobbed, his torn shirt exposing the skin of his back, which appeared bruised and scratched. What in the world had happened to him?

"Now you look here, young man," Ms. Edna commanded, stomping over to where Kenneth was now bowed at my feet, leaning over him like a scolding mother. "I will not have you comin' in here upsettin' this poor girl. You have certainly done enough as it is. I will ask ya once to leave before I go out and grab the shotgun."

Kenneth ignored her, continuing his tearful plea, wrapping his arms around my ankles.

Apparently, he had had it out with his father. After he had dropped me off at Uncle John's, he went home and started to regret his decision. He said that he never intended to abandon me there. He was always planning to return to get me. He just felt he needed some time alone to process and recover from the miscarriage. But, once home, his father began to push for him to quit his job and return to school. When he refused, the two of them came to blows, physically. He said it was the first time that his father had ever hit him. From the looks of him, his father had more than made up for the years where he didn't lay a hand on him. Kenneth appeared worn and weary. Both of his eyes were swollen and purple. He looked nearly beaten to death. Observing him was actually quite disturbing.

Eventually, Ms. Edna returned to the room. I hadn't noticed that she had left. I was too baffled yet a bit amused at the scene on the floor before me. Upon her return, she brought with her a wash bucket and warm rag, not the shotgun. To my surprise, and to Kenneth's, she gently pulled him up from the floor and began tending to his wounds. Kenneth didn't react nor resist. He simply remained still as the elderly woman bathed him. He lifted his shirt, exposing the bruises and scratches that crisscrossed over his torso and back. I winced at just the sight of them.

To my shock, Ms. Edna fixed breakfast for the three of us. Taking in the sight before me, a sight I would have sworn could have never been possible, I watched in silence as Ms. Edna and Kenneth obliged each other with light and meaningless chitchat over plates of eggs, toast, and apple slices. I sipped my coffee but didn't touch my food. I was too nervous. I was truly in awe of what I was seeing.

After breakfast, Ms. Edna cleared the table and moved out into the fields to tend to her work duties. I was left alone with Kenneth for the first time since he had abandoned me.

"Please," he began, shifting his eyes nervously over my expression, which glared back at him in a mish-mosh of disgust, pain, and sympathy. "I know I've done ya wrong, Gen. I know it. And I'm truly so very sorry. But I love ya', babe. You know that. I was just...just...scared, I guess. I should never have dropped ya off that day. Can ya please forgive me? Will ya please come back home with me?"

I stared in silence, unwilling and unable to form any words. Kenneth stared back at me, my silence causing him more obvious and visible stress.

"Please, Gen!" he begged, tears filling his eyes. "Please come back home with me."

"To where, Kenneth?" I shot back. "The barn?"

He peered at me curiously.

"Well, yeah, babe. That's our home."

I shook my head.

"No, Kenneth," I stated matter-of-factly. "I ain't leavin' here. This is my home now."

Kenneth's tearful stare quickly shaped into a cold and piercing glare.

"Ya just gonna leave me, then?" he questioned, erecting his body in the chair. "Ya just gonna let me throw it all away for nothin'? All our plans? All the things we wanted to do?"

"All the things *you* wanted to do, Kenneth," I commented. "Everything…the marriage, the barn, your plan to leave school, it was all what you wanted. I made it clear to you that I didn't want ya to quit school."

"I want ya to come back with me, Genevieve," Kenneth stated, his request more of a command.

"Please, Kenneth, just leave."

I lifted myself from my chair and pushed through the back screen door. In the distance, I could hear Kenneth slamming through the house, stomping off the front porch, and returning to whatever vehicle he had brought with him. The sound of spinning tires and an angry, growling engine could be heard fading into the distance.

Eventually, I found my way to Ms. Edna, who was busy tending to the mother hens in the chicken coop. Three of them had a fresh nest of babies. I smiled as I neared them.

"So, I take it he wanted ya to go back home with him?" Ms. Edna asked, not looking up from her chores.

"Yeah," I confirmed, lifting one of the baby chicks in my hand.

"And I take it you said no?" she continued, looking back at me over her shoulder.

"Yup," I stated, nuzzling the warm, fuzzy bird with my nose.

"Good," I heard her say, perhaps more to herself than to me.

I spent the rest of that Saturday assisting Ms. Edna with her household and farm chores before tending to my own. I was happy here. This was where I both wanted and needed to be. Ms. Edna was there for me in a way my momma could not be, even if she wanted to be.

That night, Ms. Edna, Janice, and I all sat out on the front porch, watching the stars. I listened as the two old women revisited memories from their past, simple farm stories, or tales of Ms. Edna's days as principal. I admired their bond. I was both inspired and saddened by it. On one hand, these two women had each other and a lifetime of memories to draw upon. On the other, Janice was fading, her mind and ability to care for herself becoming more and more of an issue. Still, their love was clear and could be experienced by just witnessing them interact. I felt myself longing for that kind of bond and companionship. It was then that I realized I had never had an inkling of that with Kenneth. Only lust and desire. It was in the midst of that peaceful evening that I let go of any feelings I had for him for good.

***

MOMMA WAS SUPPOSED TO visit the following weekend but couldn't. At the last minute, her new temporary assistant manager called out, something to do with his sick wife, so Momma was forced to remain in Gatlinburg. I was disappointed, but not surprised. The gaps between Momma's visits, even before she had begun covering for Mr. Barnes as head manager, were becoming larger and more consistent. There was a time when I would see her every few days. Now I was lucky to see her once a month.

Uncle John stopped by on a Wednesday evening. Ms. Edna was cautious and watchful of him, but she allowed us our time alone. I wasn't quite sure why Ms. Edna was so defensive against Uncle John. Was she aware of the history between him and my momma? How would she know that? Had Momma told her? Was it common knowledge to the older folks around these hills? I could only wonder.

"So how ya been feelin' lately?" Uncle John asked, nervously thumping his work boots over the porch floorboards. "Heard anything from Kenneth?"

"Yeah," I answered, placing a hand on Uncle John's knee to signal an end to his nervous movement. He obliged.

"He came by here a couple weeks ago. He was a mess. I guess he got into it with his daddy. He begged for me to go back with him. I refused though."

Uncle John didn't look at me. He continued to stare at the floor.

"I feel good about my decision," I continued. "I mean, I did love him...or thought I was in love with him. But I think it was more of a crush than anything. It was more..."

I stopped short; I could feel Uncle John becoming uneasy next to me.

"Sexual?" he asked, reigniting his nervous foot thumping.

I didn't respond.

We sat together on the front porch until the sun had long set. The smell of Ms. Edna preparing dinner could be enjoyed as it filtered through the front screen door.

Uncle John was never at ease during the entire visit. When he wasn't fidgeting somehow, he was nervously darting his eyes into the distance. For some reason, he was afraid to keep eye contact with me.

Just before Ms. Edna announced dinner, Uncle John returned to his old, beat-up pickup and drove off into the night. I waved as he flashed me a half-grin, taking in the sight of his dim-red brake lights as they faded into the soft mist of the night.

Janice didn't eat with us. She was going through another one of her episodes. When she was at her worst, she wouldn't come inside the cabin. She would perform her daily tasks around the farm and then return to the barn the moment the sun began to set. Ms. Edna would always ensure that Janice had plenty to eat and drink out there, but she knew better than to try to force her to join us at the dinner table. In time, she would rebound and reappear in the kitchen on her own accord. But, for the time being, Ms. Edna and I both knew better than to try to get her to do anything she wasn't willing to.

A few nights later, Janice woke me up again, shotgun in hand, a panicked yet focused look plastered over her wrinkled and withered face.

"They here again," she whispered, her eyes wide and unblinking.

Once again, my heart began to race. I sat up on the cot, gripping the quilt close to my chest.

"I don't see anything," I whispered back, squinting my eyes in the dark toward the front window.

"They just out in the woods. They just got here."

Confused, I looked at Janice. "Got here? Like, by car or somethin'?"

Janice shot me an annoyed glance. "This ain't no jokin' matter, girl," she hissed, still whispering. "They landed their spaceship just out beyond the tree line. Same place they always land. The clearing they have marked off."

I decided it was best not to ask any more questions. It was obvious she was having another episode.

For nearly fifteen minutes, Janice and I remained still in the dark, our eyes glued to the living room window. Eventually, I needed to pee, so I excused myself to the outhouse.

"I'll go with ya," Janice offered, trailing behind me, shotgun in hand.

We journeyed the short distance between the back of the cabin and the small outhouse. I peed, wiped, and was just heading back to the house when I saw it: the glow, the same eerie orange light that had appeared to Kenneth and me on the railroad tracks a few months prior.

"See," Janice whispered, keeping her eyes locked on the forest, her knuckles white as she squeezed the barrel of the gun.

Nervous and a bit scared, I urged Janice to follow me back inside the house. She didn't move.

"Janice," I whispered loudly. "Come on, let's get back inside."

She wouldn't budge.

I moved to grab her arm and pull it toward me, when I saw the orange glow become brighter in her eyes. I turned my head to see the tree line ablaze with the light. I felt my mouth open and my pulse accelerate from what I saw. There, just a bit beyond the trees, were three small figures, thin, narrow bodies and bulbous heads, standing side by side, appearing to stare out at us. One of the figures moved, and there was an intense and immediate ringing from behind my ears, the same familiar ring I had experienced several times before. I couldn't help but press both hands against the sides of my head.

"They comin'," Janice whispered, slowly aiming the shotgun. "They comin' for ya."

I felt tears of fear begin to glaze over my face.

"Get down!" Janice hollered, her face aglow in the fiery orange.

I dropped to the ground just as she fired a shot. Then another. Followed by another.

I could hear Ms. Edna screaming something from the cabin, but it was muffled by the sound of deafening thunder, followed by a blinding flash of white light. I opened my eyes and the ringing disappeared.

Before me was darkness. The orange glow was gone, but so was Janice. I jumped to my feet and bolted for the back screen door.

"What happened?" Ms. Edna asked as I fell into the kitchen.

"I saw 'em!" I cried. "Ms. Edna, the little men in the trees! I saw 'em! They real! They took Janice!"

"What do ya mean *they took Janice*?" Ms. Edna asked, opening the screen door and venturing outside.

"Wait!" I screamed, following behind her.

Together, Ms. Edna and I searched every inch of the farm property. Every coop, shed, loft, the barn, each and every single place Janice could possibly be. Gone. She had vanished. There was absolutely no sign of her whatsoever.

Eventually, we succumbed to exhaustion, both physical and emotional, and returned to the cabin for the rest of the night. I lay beside Ms. Edna, too terrified to be alone, never mind sleep.

A few hours later, just as the sun had begun to rise above the treetops, Ms. Edna and I resumed our search. We had both managed an hour or so of slumber, if that. It was enough to recharge us for another bout of searching for Janice. Ms. Edna took the front end of the property, while I combed the back half. I found myself in the woods, just beyond the tree line, in the area where I had seen the mysterious little men just hours before. As terrified as I was, I couldn't help but venture there. After a short walk, I came to a clearing, the one Janice had mentioned. Each of the surrounding trees appeared to be burnt, nearly scorched. The ground was scoured, and from what I could see, the markings appeared to form some kind of pattern. The entire area was cold and eerie. I ran back into the open fields of the farm property just as fast as my feet would carry me.

When the sun began to set that evening, we had still not found Janice. We looked everywhere, over and over again. Ms. Edna was completely beside herself. I did everything I could to provide her some form of encouragement and comfort. I promised her we would somehow find Janice. I did all the cooking and cleaning for the one meal we did sit down for. In the end, I was anxious and horrified beyond words. What was happening? What did I see in the trees last night? Were these really visitors from another world? Were they really here for me? Had they taken Janice? I don't think I slept much at all that night. I found myself fading in and out of restless bouts of unconsciousness and incredibly real and vivid nightmares. Three days later, we would finally find Janice.

***

ON THE EVENING OF the fourth day after Janice's disappearance, one of the nearby neighbors drove up to the cabin. Now, when I say nearby, I am talking seven or so miles away. Fred Burns was a tall man. He looked to be in his mid- to late fifties. He had a wife, two grown children, and seven hunting dogs. I knew this because he had visited once when I had first moved in with Ms. Edna and Janice. He was a kind man, caring toward the two aging women. He made it clear that his wife was no fan of theirs, mostly due to the long-standing rumors surrounding them, but Fred felt it was his Christian duty to look out for the ladies, at least to check in on them from time to time.

This time, though, Fred appeared nervous and perhaps frightened. He didn't bother with niceties or casual chitchat. He had Ms. Edna throw on a coat and work boots and follow him to his truck. I joined them, jumping into the back of his rust-colored Ford pickup, holding on for dear life as Fred barreled the old truck toward his farm.

He didn't say too much about why we were being taken there, but the answer was clear the moment we arrived. In plain view from the driveway of his farmhouse was the sight of Janice, stark naked, walking around the side of one of Fred's crops. Fred's wife, Rebecca, stood on the front porch, her arms crossed, her face pinched in a disapproving scowl.

"We found her this way about an hour ago," Fred told Ms. Edna, who couldn't get out of Fred's truck fast enough. "She won't respond to anything we say to her. She just keeps mumblin' somethin' in gibberish. I tried wrappin' her in a blanket, but she became pretty combative with me. I didn't know what else to do but to come and fetch ya."

Ms. Edna didn't reply. She simply started jogging out into the field toward Janice. In all the time I had known her, I had never once seen Ms. Edna move so agilely and quickly. I could tell her emotional state of panic was overpowering any sort of physical pain or ailment that would usually be a preventative burden. Fearing my presence may initiate another one of Janice's episodes, I remained near the farmhouse with the Burnses. I could feel Mrs. Burns glaring at me. I was in no mood to deal with any sort of drama, so I simply ignored her, keeping my eyes locked on the sight of Ms. Edna retrieving Janice.

With a still-mumbling Janice tightly wrapped in an old brown piece of burlap that Mr. Burns had provided, Ms. Edna escorted her visibly confused longtime companion to the passenger side of Fred's old truck. Fred hesitated after Ms. Edna closed the truck door, securing Janice inside.

"There's somethin' else you should see, Edna," Fred announced.

Ms. Edna didn't say a word as she and I followed Fred toward his barn.

Inside was chaos. Each of his pens had been opened and livestock was running and roaming everywhere. He directed us to the back corner, to the one pen that was still locked. Inside it were three goats, all male, all sedated.

"I had to drug 'em," Fred confessed, standing at the edge of the pen. "They've all been castrated. Clean. Nearly surgical. I ain't never seen anything like it."

"Fred," Ms. Edna said, shaking her head, "I ain't got time for this now. I need to get Janice back home and—"

"Janice did this," Fred declared, his eyes wide with the same look of nervousness and fear he had arrived at the cabin with. "That was how I found her. I heard my goats cryin' somethin' fierce. I ran out here and found Janice. She was just finishin' up with the third one when I caught her. I don't know how she didn't kill 'em. There wasn't even a drop of blood to be found. She simply castrated them clean and dry, almost in some kinda inhuman way. Like she was a machine or somethin'."

The three of us stared at the goats, who returned our gaze with watery, drug-heavy eyes.

No one spoke as we returned to the truck. I jumped in the back, and Ms. Edna and Fred joined Janice in the front cab.

It would be hours before Ms. Edna would speak another word.

***

"WHAT DO YA THINK happened?" I asked Ms. Edna as we sat for dinner later that evening. "Has Janice ever done that to an animal before?"

Ms. Edna was quiet for a while before she finally decided to speak. "I've never seen her do that, no," she answered, keeping her eyes focused on her plate. I watched as she angrily poked at her meal with her fork. She took several large bites before dropping the fork to the table.

"I'm really frightened, Genevieve," she said, teardrops dotting under her eyes. "I'm afraid I won't be able to take care of Janice much longer. She's gonna need some professional care."

"But, Ms. Edna," I interjected. "Janice was taken. Those men in the trees. She vanished with them. They musta left her out at Fred's farm and—"

"Enough, Genevieve!" Ms. Edna snapped, locking my eyes with a cold stare. "No such thing happened. She was havin' an episode and ran out through the backwoods and ended up over at the Burnses' farm. No spacemen put her there. She managed to get there all on her own. Lord knows how long she lingered in them woods before makin' it there. God only knows what she's been through."

I decided not to say anything more. I knew what I saw that night, and I knew that Janice vanished after that loud crack of thunder and flash of light. She couldn't have run into the woods that quickly. I would have seen her. In just a matter of a second or two, she went from standing right before me, firing a gun, to completely gone as if she had never been there at all. I could tell that Ms. Edna was just scared and confused, trying her damnedest to make sense of it all. In the end, Janice was found seven miles away without clothing, having surgically castrated three of our neighbors' goats. Regardless of how she got there, that part of the story was perhaps the most disturbing bit.

Momma would arrive the next day, unexpectedly and without notice. There was never a time when I was so happy to see my mother.

***

"WHAT ARE YA SAYIN', Gen?" Momma asked as we rounded the corner near the south side of the barn. "She was missin' for three whole days?"

"Momma," I started, the panic and fear in my voice evident. "I saw it myself. There was this orange glow out here in the trees."

I pointed to the area. We were just about to approach it.

"There was these little figures standin' just within the woods. They was watchin' us. One of 'em moved and there was a flash of light and a loud sound. Then Janice was gone. Vanished. Outta thin air."

Momma didn't say a word. We continued to walk in silence until we were just about to approach the front side of the cabin.

"Listen," she finally said, turning me to face her, "I'm gonna take some time off. I'm gonna come home. I'm gonna take ya with me. We'll be back at our place, just the two of us. We'll watch TV, go into town. Hell, perhaps we'll even take us a girl's trip over into Knoxville. Whaddya say?"

I smiled and nodded.

"I'd love that, Momma," I said, pressing my face into her hand.

"Mr. Barnes should be comin' back later in the week. I'm just gonna tell him I need this time for myself. He'll have to understand."

Momma stayed for dinner, never mentioning Janice nor what I had told her during our walk. I think it scared her. Momma didn't like these stories of night terrors and strange beings in the trees. I think she was beginning to doubt her decision to leave me out here with Ms. Edna and Janice. I could tell she was more anxious and short with Ms. Edna than she had been in the past.

Ms. Edna and I waved as Momma pulled her old car toward the direction of the dark mountain road that would take her back to Gatlinburg. Much to my surprise, Momma kept her word and reappeared just four days later to take me home with her. As much as I really didn't want to leave Ms. Edna alone with Janice at a time such as this, I went anyway. I knew I needed to be alone with my momma for a while. Of course, Ms. Edna understood and encouraged the time away. Still, had I known what was to happen next, I would have never left these two women, who I now considered my family, at all.

***

THE FIRST THREE DAYS with Momma were like a dream. As if sisters, we laughed, joked, told stories, played games, watched television, cooked, baked, and went on long walks; it was heaven. It was perhaps the first time since I was very young that Momma was with me for more than just a few days at a time. For as long as I could remember, Momma spent most of her time in Gatlinburg, leaving me mostly to fend for myself, with the nearby watchful eye of my uncle.

Uncle John joined us for dinner on the evening of the third day. Together, we laughed and enjoyed one another's company. There was no talk of Momma and Uncle John's past, not a mention of my night terrors, recent odd events with Ms. Edna and Janice, my miscarriage, or my breakup with Kenneth. We just lived and enjoyed the moment, not a care nor worry burdening our minds.

I was alone on the front porch with Uncle John while he smoked a cigarette. His demeanor had changed, and he had suddenly become quiet and withdrawn.

"What's the matter, Uncle John?" I asked, leaning beside him on the front porch railing.

He didn't answer. Instead, he took another large mouthful of smoke, expelling it with a labored, heavy sigh.

"Ya know I love ya, Gen, right?" he asked suddenly after several long minutes of complete silence.

"Of course, Uncle John," I answered, moving closer to him. "I've never doubted that, not even for a second."

He took another long drag of his cigarette.

"You a great girl, Gen," he eventually said. Several more drawn-out minutes of silence filled the air between us. "I hope ya can forgive me."

He didn't wait for my response. He smashed the cigarette against his leather belt and flicked it out into the yard behind the porch banister. In a flash, he was gone, well on his way down the worn-out pathway that would lead him back to his cabin.

I returned inside the house, assisting Momma with the dinner cleanup. Had I known what I was to discover in just a few short hours, I would have enjoyed these final moments of temporary peace far more than I did.

***

IT WAS AROUND THREE p.m. the next day when Momma sent me down to Uncle John's. She wanted to borrow some fresh eggs, something Uncle John always had a steady wealth of due to his on-site chicken coop. I felt a cold air surround me as I bounded up the front steps of his cabin. It was odd, given the midafternoon heat. It took several seconds for the sunlight to expel the darkness from inside the cabin, several seconds that seemed to move in slow motion inside my mind. First, I saw the kitchen table and nearby iron stove, all covered in various pots, pans, plates, and newspaper. Then, the sofa came into view, piles of clothing, books, a shotgun, and even more newspaper cluttering every inch. It was when my eyes focused on the bed that my pulse began to race and the room around me began to spin. There was Uncle John, lying peacefully over his handsewn quilt, his face blue, his eyes open, a syringe dangling from one of his forearm veins.

"Uncle John!" I screamed, shaking him as hard as I could. "Uncle John!"

I pressed my hand to his chest. I could feel his heart beating, but his breathing was soft and shallow. I ran as fast I could back home, screaming for Momma as soon as I was in earshot.

Together, we piled him into the backseat of Momma's old Buick and journeyed to the nearest hospital, some forty or so minutes away.

***

MOMMA AND I RETURNED home nearly twelve hours later. Exhausted, we both dropped onto Momma's bed and fell asleep as soon as our heads met the pillows. I awoke around ten-thirty later that morning and decided to return to Uncle John's cabin. He had overdosed on morphine. He was in a coma. For the first time in my life, I was close to losing someone very dear to me. I didn't know my father, but I also didn't experience his or anyone else's death. As far as I knew, my father was still out there somewhere. At least, that was what I fantasized. I knew Momma and I would be heading back up to the hospital as soon as she was awake and dressed, but I felt the need to tidy up Uncle John's place before we went. I wanted it to be perfect for him when we brought him back home. I believed in my heart that he would wake up. The doctors never said he couldn't or wouldn't, but I just felt it in my core. My Uncle John was going to come home, and I was going to be sure it was ready for him when that time came.

I managed to clean the kitchen, scrubbing every pot and pan, washing and drying every rogue dish and piece of old silverware. I didn't notice the note at first, not until I had completely situated the mess on the sofa. But when I did, I knew immediately it was going to change my life forever. The minutes I spent reading and rereading the words scrawled by my uncle's own hand across the faded yellow notepad caused my heart to ache, my head to spin, and my soul to weep. I don't know how much time passed before Momma found me, but she knew right away, just by taking once fast glance at my face, that my entire world had suddenly crumbled from beneath me.

Dear Gen,

I am addressing this letter to you because I just know you will be the one to find me. First, I just want you to know how much I love you. I always have, ever since the day you were born and I first laid eyes on you. Unfortunately, I have failed you in more ways than I can ever truly accept. I know you are aware of my issue, but I don't think anyone is fully aware of just how bad it's become. I'm a morphine addict. I have been for years. Dr. Reynolds provides it, but not in the way a good doctor should. He supplies my fix. He ensures I remain an addict. I don't blame him. It's what I asked of him, but in the end, the cost was invaluable. The cost was you. For several months, I turned a blind eye to what Dr. Reynolds was doing to you. He never said it, but I knew just enough to know he was drugging and having his way with you. The nights I'd find you in the woods, the night terrors and things you've been experiencing, it was all him. He'd press some cloth to your mouth that would cause you to pass out, and he'd have his way. I know this because I saw him with the cloth and a small bottle several times. I never asked what it was, but he'd always take it with him when he left my cabin, after I'd doped myself enough to completely go out of it. I've thought about killing him more times than I can even count. I've thought of where I'd bury him, so far in the woods that he'd never be found. But, in the end, I always chose my fix. I am at the point where I can't live without it. It's been this way for a long time. Please, tell your momma I'm sorry. Sorry for what I've done to her in the past. Sorry for failing her now. And sorry for leaving you two behind. Knowing your momma, though, I'd imagine after hearing all this, she would rather me be dead anyway. Most of all, Gen, I am sorry for what I've done to you. I promised to always be there to protect you, but I failed. I betrayed you, your momma, and God himself. I allowed some sick man to take advantage of my one and only niece simply because he took care of my addiction. I just can't live with this anymore. The guilt has been eating me alive ever since your momma took you to live with them old ladies. I'm sorry, Gen. I pray you'll forgive me. I'll suffer eternity in hell for what I've done, and I'll gladly accept that fate. I've earned it. It's what I deserve. But I pray to all things good and mighty that you will find it in your heart to forgive me and will keep some form of love for me in your memory. No matter what, I have never not loved you. I just failed you. Live on, Gen. Do right. Do good. Love your momma, but most of all, love you, dear sweet girl. Have your momma have me cremated and scattered at the back edge of our property. It's up to her on what to do with the cabin and all. I love you, Gen. Please, always know that. I've always loved you.

Uncle John

***

THE NEXT SEVERAL HOURS consisted of endless questioning by James Haviland, Sevier County Sheriff; questions that were crude, invasive, and embarrassing. I was to be taken in for examination, my virtue under question. Momma interjected and interfered so much that one of the three deputies that had arrived with Sherriff Haviland had to escort her outside, even though all she did was show them Uncle John's suicide note, which, thank God, from last accounts, he was still alive, although still in a coma. I hadn't had time to process the information Uncle John had relayed in his note. It was too all-consuming and too heavy to absorb in one sitting. As soon as Momma read the note, she phoned the sheriff and whisked me back to the house. She didn't speak a word of what the letter said until the sheriff and his deputies arrived.

"Did ya ever see Dr. Reynolds during these experiences?" Sheriff Haviland asked, shifting some chewing tobacco with this tongue. "I mean, I'm gonna need more to go on here than just some junkie's suicide note. Dr. Reynolds is a revered and respected man. I can't just go up and arrest him based on just this one accusation. I'm gonna need further proof and evidence, and unless you can recall seeing him doin' some of what your uncle is accusin' him of doin', then, I'm sorry, hon, but there ain't much I can do here."

I felt dizzy. My head was spinning. I wasn't able to fully comprehend all that was being asked of me, even less what was casually being stated. I had never seen Dr. Reynolds here. Not ever. My only encounters with him had been at his house while I was living there with Kenneth. As far as I could remember, I had never once seen him anywhere near our house or Uncle John's cabin.

The intense questioning went on for another half hour or so before Sheriff Haviland finally concluded that the only thing that could be done was to have me examined and perhaps take Dr. Reynolds in for questioning. Nothing was certain, and nothing was promised.

I could hear Momma arguing with the sheriff as he and his deputies made their way back to their vehicles. One by one, I heard the three law enforcement cars speed off down the gravel driveway and out onto the nearby country road. Momma returned inside the house, broken and defeated.

"I can't goddamn believe this!" she shouted the moment she was fully back inside the house. "I have a damn written confession about what's been goin' on around here, and the man who claims to serve and protect us mountain folk won't make a simple arrest. I swear it, had this been one of us accused of such a thing, ya better believe the ol' sheriff would be out here makin' arrests faster than one could even figure out what was happenin'."

She dropped her eyes to mine. I was still seated at the kitchen table, the plate Sheriff Haviland had been eating from still in place at the spot where he had been sitting across from me during the interview; an interview that went on for far too long and felt far more like an interrogation than a sympathetic conversation with a victim.

"I'm so very sorry, Gen," Momma sobbed, dropping to her knees as she neared me. "I'm sorry…I'm sorry…"

I moved to embrace her. Together on the kitchen floor, we cried; a mother and daughter wrapped in each other's arms, the pain between them profound and understood.

***

MOMMA FINALLY RETURNED TO the motel three days later. I had to beg her to allow me to go back to Ms. Edna's. Momma wanted me with her in Gatlinburg, but I was determined to finish out the rest of my homeschooling. According to Ms. Edna, if we continued the progress we had been making, I would be eligible for a diploma in less than a year's time, far earlier than I would have been had I been able to remain at Sevierville High. She was going to speak with Principal Lindsay. There was a slight possibility I was going to be allowed to walk with my class when the time came. There were no promises, so I didn't hold on to any one specific scenario. It would be nice to receive a diploma alongside my former classmates, but it was no longer a relevant concern in my life.

Uncle John was still in a coma. I had no way to get to the hospital after Momma had returned to Gatlinburg. Momma continued to receive updates via phone calls from the doctors and nurses, and she would in turn relay the information to me through nightly calls to Ms. Edna's.

I didn't speak of the letter Uncle John had left and what it claimed was the truth. There was no doubt that Uncle John was an addict and that he had indeed attempted suicide, but the details concerning Dr. Reynolds's involvement just remained far too unbelievable to me. Dr. Reynolds had not been very kind to me during my time living with his son under the Reynolds family roof, but I simply could not imagine nor accept that he had drugged and raped me for months. I didn't know what to believe anymore. At this point, the prospect of alien abduction was far more understandable and acceptable to me.

My days consisted of the regular routine: morning chores, the homeschool lessons, lunch, more lessons, evening chores, dinner, followed by some downtime with the two women. Ms. Edna would no longer allow Janice to reside in the barn loft. After her disappearance, Janice was different. She was far calmer and more peaceful. She no longer spoke of the mysterious men in the woods nor their involvement in my life. When she did speak, it was of old memories of days long gone. My favorite time of the day was listening to the two women recount the tales of their youth. For mountain women, they were wise and worldly. They had even traveled outside of Appalachia several times, going as far north as Canada and as far south as Mexico. I envied their experiences.

After a week back at Ms. Edna's, Momma showed up unexpectedly.

"Come on," she hollered from her car window, the engine still running. "We haveta get to the hospital."

I said a quick goodbye to Ms. Edna and Janice before joining Momma in the car. Momma didn't say another word until we were a good ten minutes into the drive.

"They gonna take Uncle John off the machines today," she stated plainly, without any emotion whatsoever.

"What does that mean?" I asked quietly, my voice quickly filling with a wealth of anxiety.

"It means..." Her voice trailed into tears. "It means he needs to be able to breathe on his own."

I waited for a moment before questioning further.

"And if he doesn't?"

Momma kept her eyes fixed firmly out the windshield. More tears began to glaze her skin as she readied her response. "It means he isn't gonna make it, Gen."

I turned my head just as my own tears began to flood my face. Together in our separate silences, Momma and I cried the entire rest of the journey to the county hospital.

***

THE SIGHT OF UNCLE John lying on the hospital bed, tubes protruding from his nose and mouth, his eyes sealed shut, his face sunken and hollow, was always terrifying. He looked far worse now than he had the night we first brought him here. His skin looked drier and less hydrated, and his body appeared frailer and more fragile. Momma and I waited together in the room for the doctors to finally arrive, a group of three that would initiate the removal of the tubes.

"I want ya to know that despite what I told ya about what occurred between your uncle and me as children, it has nothin' to do with you," Momma stated, brushing back some of the hair that fell across Uncle John's forehead. "Your uncle loved ya, Gen. Very, very much."

I nodded, tears still streaming down my face.

"And despite what he said in that note and what is more than likely the truth of what has been goin' on with ya…"

I looked up as Momma struggled to gather her words.

"Well, despite that, he loved ya. This is why we are here now. His love for you was stronger than his addiction. He couldn't live with the guilt of what he had done. He couldn't bear the fact that he had failed ya…that he had failed me in failing you."

I didn't say a word as Momma continued to move and adjust various parts of her brother. She repositioned his head, hand-brushed his hair, and realigned his arms. She did this repeatedly until it appeared she felt certain of his comfort. Despite everything, it was clear that Momma still loved her brother, and very much so.

After an hour alone in the room, the team of doctors finally arrived.

"Ms. Delany, we need you to sign these," the sole female doctor stated, handing a large clipboard to Momma.

"What is it?" Momma asked, adjusting herself in her seat.

"It's your approval that we will not attempt any resuscitation efforts if your brother is incapable of breathing on his own."

Momma just stared at the clipboard. When she finally took it, she read over the document several times before signing. The team of doctors, two older gentleman and the middle-aged female, simply went about their business of poking and prodding at Uncle John, reading and rereading the nearby charts and monitors, and mumbling amongst themselves in the corner of the room.

Finally, Momma returned the clipboard. Within a few minutes, the doctors had removed the artificial assistance that was keeping Uncle John alive, and the five of us watched and waited.

The breathing continued; the heart monitor kept its rhythmic beeping. This went on for one minute. Then two. Three, four. It was just after the five-minute mark when everything stopped. Uncle John's stomach and chest ceased to rise and fall; the heart monitor signaled a deafening, monotone, non-stop drone. He was gone. My one and only uncle, gone. I felt Momma pull me toward her. We were left alone again, the doctors mumbling various forms of apologies and regrets as they exited the room.

I cried. I sobbed. Momma just held me. I didn't see her cry again at all, not even when two orderlies arrived to remove Uncle John from the room.

A week later, he was returned to us, his remains a collection of ashes in a simple cardboard box, a plastic bag containing what was left of him. Momma didn't bother purchasing an urn. The two of us stood side by side at the edge of our family property, following Uncle John's request that his ashes be scattered there. I cried. I sobbed. Momma didn't shed another tear.

***

I WAS BACK AT Ms. Edna's. Three weeks had gone by since we lost Uncle John. Both our house and Uncle John's cabin were up for sale, along with the sizeable property that went along with them. Momma was back in Gatlinburg. I was to finish the remainder of my homeschooling and move in with her in a small one-bedroom apartment she had leased near the motel.

Aside from offering her condolences over the loss of my uncle, Ms. Edna didn't dwell on what was to come. She made an extra effort to maintain a sense of normalcy around the farm. I went about the business of performing my daily chores, alongside our lessons, keeping in tune with the melody of peace Ms. Edna was working hard to maintain.

It was a Tuesday night when Janice woke me up.

"It wasn't them who took your baby," she whispered. She had wandered from the bed she shared with Ms. Edna and to the side of my cot. "It wasn't them."

I sat up, trying hard to focus my eyes and ears.

"Janice, what?" I whispered. "Ya better get back to bed. Ms. Edna is gonna—"

"They watchin' out for ya. They ain't intendin' no harm."

On her own, Janice shuffled back toward the bedroom. I wasn't quite sure what she was referring to. I assumed it was another episode involving her fear of the mysterious men in the woods and whatnot, but for the first time, she wasn't frightful about it. She spoke plainly and peacefully, and even though her words were erratic and unbelievable, I felt a sense of comfort from them. I couldn't say why. I just did. I slipped back into sleep far faster than I had ever done following previous similar occurrences.

***

THREE DAYS LATER, KENNETH arrived at the farm. This time, he wasn't here to try to win me back. He was here in a rage.

"Your momma is a fuckin' bitch!" he screamed, slamming shut the door to a brand-new, chocolate-brown Lincoln Continental.

"Wha—" I started, but was stopped short by the fury of anger in Kenneth's words.

"She's been harrassin' the sheriff about some shit your uncle claimed about my daddy. They took my daddy down for questionin' yesterday. The newspaper picked up on it. Today's headline is about my daddy bein' accused of druggin' and rapin' an underage female."

I was standing alone on the front porch but could hear Ms. Edna shuffling toward the screen door to join me.

"Sheriff Haviland told me that girl is you!" Kenneth pointed at me the way one would point at a pile of manure they were trying to warn someone else not to step in. "It's fuckin' lies!" he screamed, his eyes red, his face crimson, the veins in his neck revealing the rate of his pulse.

"Young man," Ms. Edna interrupted, "I think ya need to find your way back home. Ain't nobody here got anything to do with—"

"Shut the fuck up, you old dyke hag!" Kenneth screamed, his face twisted and hateful.

"Hey!" I shouted, stepping toward him. "Don't talk to her that way!"

Kenneth didn't move. He only stared, his eyes radiating nothing but pure, unbridled rage.

"Ya gonna tell everyone the truth," he commanded, nodding his head at his own words. "I'm takin' ya with me and you gonna tell the sheriff and the newspapers, and anyone and everyone else that all this shit your momma is sayin' ain't nothin' but lies."

I stared back, unsure how to respond.

"Let's go," he snapped, grabbing my wrist and pulling me toward the car.

"Stop!" a voice shouted from behind us.

Turning our heads in unison, Kenneth, Ms. Edna, and I all stared in a state of shock as Janice appeared from behind a nearby tree, some sort of blade in each hand.

Kenneth scoffed and continued to move toward the car.

"I said stop!" Janice screamed in a nearly otherworldly voice, jumping at Kenneth, slicing the side of his shirt. Kenneth dropped my arm and turned his attention to the tear in his clothing.

"You crazy old bitch! Ya coulda sliced me open!"

"Next time, I will. Now, go on outta here. Ya leave this girl alone, ya hear?"

Kenneth stared at Janice, his anger now a mixture of confusion and disbelief.

"This ain't over yet, Genevieve," Kenneth yelled, reprising his disgusted pointing. "I ain't gonna allow you fuckin' hillbillies to tarnish my daddy's good name. He's worked too damn hard and long to secure his good reputation in these parts. I ain't just gonna stand by and let some no-good whore and her slut of a daughter ruin that."

He didn't wait for a reply. He jumped inside the shiny new vehicle, fired the ignition, and sped off down the gravel pathway toward the mountain road that would lead him back to Sevierville.

"Ain't a bit of that true, darlin," Ms. Edna cooed as she stood by my side. "Come, let's get ya inside and fix ya up with some tea."

"Some of it's true, Ms. Edna," I began, keeping my eyes in the distance where Kenneth's brake lights were slowly fading from view. "The things about what Momma is doin'. All that is true."

Ms. Edna pulled me inside and began to prepare the tea. Janice had disappeared somewhere on the farm property.

With two streaming mugs before us, I told Ms. Edna everything: the details of Uncle John's letter, each of his confessions, including the bit about Dr. Reynolds, the lengthy and thorough portion of his confession that even I could not believe.

Ms. Edna didn't speak a word. She listened and nodded when necessary, confirming her understanding of my words, but simply sat still and sipped at her tea.

Afterward, she changed the subject, and led us to bed when the time came. Janice made her way into the cabin just as Ms. Edna and I were changing into our nightgowns. It took me at least two hours to fall asleep that night. I could only imagine the chaos and drama Momma had caused in town. The fact that the local newspaper had made the story their top headline meant it was what every single living and breathing creature that resided in Sevierville would be focused on and talking about. Thank God I was so far away from it all, cut off and disconnected from the rumor and scandal. Or so I thought.

***

THE NEXT DAY, SHERIFF James Haviland arrived. He didn't bother with niceties as he informed Ms. Edna and me as we greeted him on the front porch, that I was to be taken down to the Sevier County Sheriff's Department to continue our interview and document my official statement. Ms. Edna offered him some tea, which he bluntly refused, while I ran to fetch my shoes. Within minutes, I had joined the sheriff inside his vehicle, and we were making the journey toward Sevierville. Several long minutes of silence passed before the sheriff broke the heavy and awkward stillness between us.

"I know Kenneth Reynolds was out here yesterday," the sheriff spoke plainly, his voice a bit annoyed and cold sounding. "He shouldn'ta done that. It's bad enough this whole thing was picked up by the paper. I don't need him runnin' around makin' everything worse."

I didn't say a word. I only listened.

"Your momma is the one who called the paper. She's really makin' a huge deal of this." Sheriff Haviland sighed, turning the car onto the paved road that would take us into town.

"What this is, girl," he continued, keeping his eyes out on the road before us, "it's down to the word of a respected town citizen, not to mention the town's only doctor, and that of a dead morphine junkie with a bad reputation."

Sheriff Haviland turned to face me when he heard me struggle to catch my breath. The degrading way he had just referred to my uncle had led me to quick and instant tears.

"I'm sorry, honey. It's just the truth. Your uncle sure opened a can of worms with that note, and sad as it is, trust and respect just ain't on his side. I'm sure you are aware of his past."

Wiping my face, I stared back at the sheriff, my silence urging him to continue.

"Honey, your family was quite the scandal at one time. Your grandpappy used to have his way with both his children, your momma and uncle. When the truth finally came out, it nearly killed your grandmother. The kids dropped outta school and the family just stayed up where you've lived since you was born. Your grandpappy was alone for years in the cabin your uncle ended up livin' in. Your grandmother stayed with your momma and uncle in the house you were brought up in till her death, just before you was born. Your grandpappy died just a few months later. I believe it was the shame that killed 'em, especially when it became known that their son was doin' the same thing to his sister that had been done to him and his sister by their daddy."

My heart was pounding so loudly inside my chest that I was beginning to have trouble comprehending all that the sheriff was telling me. None of what he was saying had ever been told to me by anyone. I didn't know what to think or believe.

"Did ya not know about all this, honey?" he gave a short cackle. "I bet ya don't even know who your daddy is, do ya?"

I couldn't breathe. I began to fumble with the door handle, but Sheriff Haviland stopped the car.

"Get a hold of yourself, girl," he commanded, furrowing his brow in an annoyed and impatient scowl. "I ain't got time for all the dramatics."

It took every bit of self-control I had to appear stable. All I wanted to do was scream and cry. I had so many questions, so much to say, but I was forced into silence until we arrived at the sheriff's office.

The next four hours consisted of a barrage of questions by Sheriff Haviland. He would ask and re-ask the same questions over and over until he appeared pleased with my answers. I was no longer sure of what I was saying to him. I just wanted to leave. I didn't have the information he wanted. I couldn't clearly remember most of my night terrors, and what I did remember was too hazy to really describe, but nothing, not one single memory, ever involved Dr. Reynolds. I told the sheriff I did not believe that portion of my uncle's letter, the portion that had accused the doctor of raping me, and it seemed to please the sheriff's narrative.

According to Sheriff Haviland, Uncle John was a no-good junkie with an ax to grind. Maybe it was Dr. Reynolds who had been providing my uncle with the morphine, too much, perhaps, which was certainly unethical and illegal, but the smear and accusation against him was simply final damage by a man better off dead and forgotten. The sheriff made no secret of his clear and concise disdain for my uncle. He insulted and demeaned him at every given opportunity, and if the opportunity did not present itself, he would invent one. If there was any relief to be found, it was in the fact that the sheriff's narrative did not involve the theory that Uncle John was the one committing the drugged sexual assaults that his note had accused the doctor of. I had subconsciously feared that the sheriff would see this as a clear and obvious scenario, especially considering that he knew of my uncle's past behavior with my mother. Thankfully, he didn't go there, and that was perhaps a part of the reason why I was so willing to blindly sign his pre-prepared statement.

Starved and thirsty, Sheriff Haviland had me sign the statement, with the promise that he would take me for dinner afterward. Exhausted, ashamed, degraded, and broken, I signed the paper, never reading a single word on the page.

As promised, Sheriff Haviland took me to the nearby café, the same one I had been to with Kenneth during our first date. The bittersweet memories of it all flooded my head as the sheriff and I found a seat in the back corner of the dining area. Thankfully, much of the place was empty, only a few solo patrons scattered about here and there. No one seemed to notice or pay much attention to us.

"I'm glad you were so cooperative, hon," Sheriff Haviland announced after he had placed a food order for the both of us. "With a signed statement exonerating the doctor, this will all be sealed and done with. I'm gonna release a statement to the paper, quoting some of your statement. That should set things straight, and clear the unnecessary smoke surroundin' Dr. Reynolds."

"But I didn't write that statement," I said softly, my voice weak and parched.

"Ya signed it, hon. It's as good as done now. Your signature means those are your words."

"But I don't know for sure that what Uncle John said in that note isn't the truth. I don't remember much about those night terrors. For all I know, it could very well be what really happened. I understand my Uncle John had his issues, but I never once knew him to be a liar. To me or to anyone."

The sheriff scoffed, his eyes focused on the cup of coffee he was assaulting with far too much sugar.

"Honey, a man capable of touchin' his baby sister in a way that God never intended and then livin' most of his adult life with a needle jabbed in his arm is not worthy of any credence. I know ya loved him, but the sad truth is, he was just a man who hated himself so much that he wasn't gonna take his own life without tryin' to take down the one who had provided him his fix. He was just tryin' to bite the hand that fed him. Now, of course, we will address the negligence and legality of what Dr. Reynolds was prescribin' to your uncle, but that is another matter altogether. It has nothin' to do with the just god-awful things he was accusin' this good man of. Now that is what we must clear and handle first."

I just stared at him as he gulped down his sugar-heavy coffee.

"Your momma, well, I know she's gonna continue to be a problem, but the thing is, your statement concludes this. She's just gonna have to accept that."

We ate our meals in silence. The sheriff didn't seem interested in any form of conversation with me. He'd gotten what he was after, and as soon as he had me fed and situated, he would take me back to Ms. Edna's, uncaring and unconcerned with me for the foreseeable future.

***

MOMMA CALLED MS. EDNA'S the next evening.

"What did ya say to them, Genevieve?" she asked breathlessly into the phone. "Ya signed a statement? Did ya even read what it said? It clears Dr. Reynolds of everything! There's nothin' we can do at this point unless I hire an attorney to fight and try to get this to trial. I can't afford that, Gen! Now we got no other choice but to just accept what—"

The call went dead. Disconnected. She didn't call back. I was relieved that she didn't.

Ms. Edna didn't ask for any of the details. She knew enough. Instead, she distracted me with tales of her time at a bakers' retreat in South Georgia. I joined her as she painted the memory for me in full detail and color. I didn't coast back into the rumination of my problems until later that night, when I struggled to find the escape of slumber.

***

AFTER TWO WEEKS OF nothing but the usual routine around the farm, Momma arrived. She was calm. She didn't speak a word of the ordeal until we were alone on the walk we always seemed to take whenever she visited.

"I'm disappointed, Gen," she concluded after ranting for twenty minutes or so about the fact I had signed a statement.

"But, Momma. I just want this to go away. I ain't had a night terror in forever. Everything is fine now. I'm safe here with Ms. Edna and Janice. Why worry about all that? How do we know Uncle John was tellin' the truth anyhow?"

She shot me a cold and glaring stare. "Don't talk that way," she snapped. "Your uncle was a lot of things, but a liar certainly wasn't one of 'em. He was a true man who loved his family. His issue with the needle may have derailed him, but his love and honesty were always intact."

I didn't argue nor disagree. My silence was agreement enough for Momma.

As we neared the south side of the barn, I conjured the courage to ask Momma something that had been plaguing my mind ever since the sheriff had first mentioned it during the car ride into Sevierville.

After recounting what the sheriff had revealed to me, I was stunned when Momma didn't resist nor react to any of the words that had fallen so easily from my mouth. After several long seconds of silence, she finally spoke.

"It's true, baby," she whispered, no tears, no emotion. "And it's my fault everyone ended up knowin' about everything. I told our preacher about what Daddy had done, and he ended up tellin' the whole damn town. The shame and embarrassment was too much for us. Momma pulled us from school, and we just went to work on the farm till we was old enough to go and do our own thing. It all broke my momma's heart. She died never forgivin' my daddy."

I didn't know what to say. I could feel the immense pain radiating from my momma, but she refused to allow any of it to affect or control her demeanor. She spoke factually and a bit stoically.

"It took me years to let all that go. My daddy loved us, in his own broken way. It caused me a lifetime of pain, but I've made peace with it."

"What about Uncle John?" I finally asked after sensing a lull in her need to speak.

"I'm not sure he ever forgave Daddy. It always stayed with him. He refused to see Daddy in those last years while Daddy lived alone out in the cabin. Only Momma and I would venture down there. Daddy started to lose his mind in the year or so before he died. Even though he and Momma didn't live as a married man and woman anymore, it broke what bit of life Daddy had left when Momma passed. He was forgettin' most of us, but he never forgot Momma. He never stopped lovin' her, even though she would barely even speak to him."

"Who's my daddy?" I heard myself ask, addressing the final thing Sheriff Haviland had said, which continued to haunt me weeks later.

"I've already told ya, Gen. He ran off when you was a baby."

"I know, Momma, but who was he? What was his name?"

I could feel the energy between us become dense and locked. Momma shut down. She didn't say another word until we were back in front of the cabin.

"I'll be back next week. Ms. Edna is gonna give ya some time away from your lessons, and I wanna take ya to see the apartment in Gatlinburg. Ya gonna love it, Gen. It's so nice and new."

I just smiled and nodded. I wasn't sure why she refused to talk any further about my father, but it now had my interest and curiosity piqued to a level that I knew would not be satiated until I had the answers my heart was seeking. I think Momma could sense it as well. She kissed my cheek and piled into her old Buick. It struggled to start but eventually fired and carried her down the gravel pathway and onto the mountain road beyond.

***

THE DAY BEFORE MOMMA was to arrive to take me back to Gatlinburg with her, Kenneth Reynolds showed up again. This time, he was calm and remorseful. He brought both Ms. Edna and Janice neatly arranged bunches of wildflowers, each wrapped in ribbon. For me, he brought an enormous bouquet of bright-red roses.

"I need to apologize for my behavior the last time I was here, ladies," he confessed as the three of us stood above him on the front porch. "It was rude, uncalled for, unacceptable, and not very Christian. Please, ladies, I beg your forgiveness."

I looked to Ms. Edna, who returned my glance. I didn't know how to respond, so I waited for her to take the lead.

"Thank you, Kenneth," she finally said, turning her head back in his direction. "This is certainly appreciated. Still, it is kindly asked of you that ya please stop payin' us these unannounced visits. Genevieve is here as a student. This is not a social complex. I ask that you respect that."

Kenneth nodded, although I saw a glint of something sinister swirl in his eyes.

I agreed to speak with him alone.

Hesitantly, Ms. Edna and Janice moved inside the cabin, though I knew they were still very much within earshot. Kenneth knew it too.

"Thank you for clearin' my daddy's good name," Kenneth said brightly. "It's appreciated."

I didn't respond. I simply allowed him to speak.

"I'm sorry to hear about your Uncle John. I never had any issue with him. I thought he looked after ya well. At least, he did when it came to me."

I thanked him for his acknowledgment, even though it was something he should have expressed the last time he was here instead of the unfounded and insensitive rage he held toward me in regard to what my mother had said and done.

"I still wanna prove myself to ya, Gen," he finally whispered after several long minutes of silence transpired between us. "I can't stop thinkin' about ya. I still love ya. Please give me the chance to prove it all to ya."

I shook my head.

"No, Kenneth," I stated flatly. "It's over."

He stared at me, his expression broken and pathetic.

"For good."

My final words seemed to slap him across the face. Assuming he would become angry, I was surprised when he simply nodded, delivered a quiet and simple goodbye, and returned to his sparkling-new chocolate-brown Lincoln. I stood alone on the front porch, the massive bouquet in hand as Kenneth peeled off into the night.

***

MOMMA WAS RIGHT. THE apartment was charming. It was far newer than our house back in Locust Ridge. The kitchen was modern, the appliances all brand-new. The bathroom had a large countertop with two sinks. The toilet was standard, not a pull-chain, and the shower was a walk-in model with a fogged-glass wall. I was very impressed. I could see myself living here, although I would most certainly miss Ms. Edna and Janice tremendously.

"Whaddya think?" Momma beamed after she had taken me on a tour of the entire living space. "Once we sell everything in Locust Ridge, I'll be able to afford to decorate it better. For now, I just have the basics."

I smiled and nodded.

"It's beautiful, Momma. I love it. Congratulations."

Momma simply stared at me for a moment. I wasn't sure of her mindset as she slowly moved her eyes over each feature of my face. The quiet moment lasted a bit too long for my comfort, and I suddenly felt myself become sweaty and awkward.

"Come, let's get to the motel so Mr. Barnes can see ya. He ain't seen ya since you was about eight years old."

***

"WELL, LOOK AT YA!" Mr. Barnes exclaimed the moment he laid eyes on me. "You're a grown woman now. Wow! I can't believe it. I swear, Eva, these kids just grow up too damn fast. Look at my Derek. He's eighteen now. Seems like only yesterday I was still wipin' his ass."

I smiled shyly as Mr. Barnes continued to openly gawk and compliment me. He was a nice man. Short, overweight, and balding. He was exactly how I remembered him, perhaps a bit older looking. He was kind to Momma. He had provided her a lot of opportunity over the years. Together, they acted as co-managers. Mr. Barnes was away more often, so Momma took on more of the overall responsibilities. The downside to that meant she had even less time for me than she had before. When I moved to Gatlinburg, I would at least see her every evening.

Momma and I spent the rest of the day venturing around Gatlinburg. It was nothing like Sevierville. Gatlinburg was a bustling tourist town. Attractions, motels, hotels, restaurants, you name it. Each glittering tourist-focused attraction pulled at the eye as we wandered the streets together. The nearby Smoky Mountains towered above the town, seeming to touch the sky. It felt like I had stuck my finger into a light socket. The energy here was light-years away from the peace and quiet of Locust Ridge.

We stopped at a quaint diner for dinner. It was the first time in so long that Momma and I had enjoyed a day out in public together. For years now, most of the time I spent with her was during her rare days off, most of which she would use to clean her uniforms or catch up on much-needed rest. I enjoyed every second of our time together now. Now that I was older, I appreciated it more. I related to Momma as a woman. I sought her advice and valued her opinions. Unlike most teenage girls, I missed out on the rebellious phase against my mother. Perhaps, had she been around more, I would have spent a few years detesting and challenging everything Momma said and did, but since she was always a distant figure, I cherished and relished having her around whenever possible.

We didn't speak of Uncle John, the note, the statement, Dr. Reynolds, or even Ms. Edna and Janice. Like two schoolgirls, we laughed, gossiped, window-shopped, and then ended the night side by side on Momma's new sofa, watching reruns of *I Love Lucy*. For the first time in weeks, I was truly relaxed and at peace. I fell asleep against Momma, who later moved to her bed, ensuring I was covered with a thick blanket, my head resting against an extra pillow.

***

"THIS IS DEREK," MOMMA announced. "He's Mr. Barnes's eldest son."

I felt myself blush as Derek took my hand in his. He was gorgeous, by far the most handsome and attractive young man I had ever laid eyes on. My reaction to him was one of innocent allure, not the sexual appeal I had experienced with Kenneth. Sure, Derek was absolutely appealing in that same physical way, but for whatever reason, my mind didn't go there, and my body didn't flush with arousal. I was simply at ease in his presence, although nervous and a bit awkward.

"Wow, you are just as beautiful as your momma said you were," Derek declared, pressing his soft pink lips to the skin of my fingers. "It is a most certain pleasure to finally meet ya, Ms. Genevieve."

"I know I'm supposed to be off," Momma interjected, a huge, jovial smile plastered over every single inch of her expression, "but I'm gonna run through some inventory lists with Mr. Barnes. It'll only take an hour, tops. Then we can go get some lunch and continue our day."

I nodded, and Momma followed Mr. Barnes into the motel's office, leaving me alone with Derek.

"How long ya in town for?" he asked, his light-brown hair fluttering in the wind.

"Just a week," I answered, now a bit calmer and more composed.

"I'd love to spend some time with ya while you're here," Derek suggested. "If that's alright with you and your momma."

I smiled and looked away. "I'd like that," I managed to squeak.

"Great," Derek continued. "I'll ask your momma if she's okay with it and what time would be good. I'll see ya soon, Ms. Genevieve."

He kissed my fingers again before strutting off down the sidewalk. His black leather jacket caught the sunlight; his perfectly fit jeans bulged in all the right places. Still, I wasn't excited nor physically heated in the way I had been when I was first around Kenneth. I suppose a few years of fantasizing had something to do with it. After it happened, though, and I got to know the real man behind the beautiful exterior, the clarity of my attraction became known. I lusted for Kenneth. I never really loved him. So, in a way, my feeling about meeting Derek was more refreshing. There was something more to it. I simply wanted to spend some time with him and get to know him better. Images of his imagined naked body never crossed my mind. Maybe I was maturing. I didn't bother to try to provide myself an impossible answer.

***

TWO DAYS LATER, DEREK, dressed in a form-fitting, button-down, short-sleeved shirt and painted-on jeans, arrived at the apartment for our date. Ever respectful and considerate, he had asked Momma's permission to take me out. She was excited and honored, gleefully granting her blessing and suggesting a free evening. Immediately, she took me shopping for a dress, a soft floral print that was both summery and comfortable. As much as I had appreciated having Susan Bellman, the Sevierville dress shop owner, help me in preparation for my first date with Kenneth, having Momma paint my lips and curl my hair was a comforting, welcoming experience. I enjoyed getting ready just as much as I did the date.

Derek was a perfect gentleman. He was smart and interesting. He was curious about me and my life back in Locust Ridge. He didn't dominate the conversation; he didn't focus solely on himself, and he insisted that I have as much speaking time as he did. It was new and refreshing. Although Kenneth had been perfectly enjoyable during our first few encounters, the latter days with him still dominated my thinking, so having a different experience with a new young man was not only pleasurable, but much needed.

We rode the chairlift at Ober Gatlinburg, a wintertime ski resort and mostly year-round amusement park. We played the games, rode the slides, consumed the sweets; it was a perfect evening.

Dropping me back off at the apartment, Derek kissed my fingers and upper wrist, signaling his further interest. I smiled and returned a kiss to his cheek. I even saw him blush in the faint glow of the small light next to the door of Momma's apartment.

Once I was back inside, Momma wanted every single detail of the night. I entertained her excitement with a play-by-play account of the evening. Momma squealed and giggled as though she were a fourteen-year-old when I told her of the front-door goodbye kiss. Momma was not only enthusiastically supportive of a possible relationship between Derek and me, but she was also personally involved and invested. It felt good to have Momma so close by and so excited about my life. Locust Ridge felt so far away now. A part of me really didn't want to go back. I stewed over the idea of asking Momma if I could just quit my studies with Ms. Edna. I knew she'd never go for it, and deep down, I knew that wasn't what I really wanted either. Still, it was great to know I had the potential of a very bright, new, and exciting life waiting for me here in Gatlinburg as soon as my homeschooling was through. I fell asleep that night knowing my days in Locust Ridge were numbered, and peaceful in accepting the fact that I would most likely never go back there again once I was fully settled here with Momma.

***

"KENNETH HAS BEEN OUT here three times since you've been gone," Ms. Edna admitted not ten minutes into our first conversation upon my return. Momma had stayed for supper before heading back to Gatlinburg. I missed her already, but I knew my future would be waiting with her there, now just less than a year away.

"What did he want?" I asked, nervous yet a bit uncaring as to the details.

"You, hon," Ms. Edna answered, helping me unpack my laundry.

"Janice had to chase him outta here again with those blades of hers. You'd think that boy would be scared outta his wits by some crazy old mountain woman chasin' him down with objects that could kill him. Hell, she already sliced open his shirt that time, and I'm afraid she'll actually hurt him, but there ain't much I can do to stop her once she gets after him. I told him that and warned him his life was in his own hands each time he ventured up here."

"Did he ask where I was?"

"Of course," Ms. Edna nodded.

"Did ya tell him?"

"Now, honey, do ya think for a second I'm that stupid?" she asked, placing her hands on her hips. "I told him it was none of his damn business where ya were and to never come back here again."

"But he still came back?"

"Yes, each time with flowers though. I swear, you'd think someone died around here with all the bouquets we've collected."

In that moment, I knew Kenneth would return. I dreaded it but mentally prepared myself for it.

***

AS EXPECTED, KENNETH SHOWED up two days later. It was a Friday evening. He was dressed up.

"I'm here to ask ya to a movie," he announced, offering me another large bouquet of roses. This time, the arrangement was yellow. They were beautiful, but I rejected them.

"No, Kenneth," I said boldly. "I am refusin' both your offer and your flowers. I have made it clear to you more than once now that I have absolutely no interest in ya anymore. Please, just stop. Please, just leave me alone."

I could feel Ms. Edna's presence behind me. I had told her to wait just inside the cabin near the screen door. She had the shotgun in case Kenneth became belligerent.

Instead, he started to cry. Weep, even. He fell to his knees on the gravel driveway, his shoulders heaving, his voice moaning. I didn't react. I remained still on the front porch, viewing his pathetic begging as an uninvested spectator. Eventually, he rose to his feet, his tears slowly ceasing.

"I'm so sorry for everything I did to hurt ya, Gen," he stuttered, his voice weak and broken by still-drizzling tears. "I pray every night to the good Lord above that you will find it in your heart to forgive me and provide me another chance to make ya happy."

I didn't respond. It didn't matter what I said, how I said it, or how much I said it, Kenneth would never listen to me. He only heard what he wanted to hear and refused to accept my decision as a final answer.

Defeated, he retreated to his Lincoln Continental and slowly pulled down the pathway to the main road. I suppose he was hoping I would stop him, but I spun around and returned inside the cabin.

***

THREE WEEKS LATER, MOMMA arrived. She had sold everything: our house, Uncle John's cabin, and the surrounding properties. Thrilled at the selling price, especially considering the fact that she had inherited everything, Momma was eager for the profit. We had lunch with Ms. Edna; Janice was out somewhere on the farm. I crammed a bag with enough clothing to last the weekend. I was heading with Momma to pack up all our things. The closing on the sale would be in another week.

The first day, we spent the entire time cleaning and clearing our old home. Filling three giant black trash bags with old paperwork and junk, we concluded boxing whatever valuables were left and aligned them near the front door. Momma had decided to leave the furniture with the house. It was old and broken down anyway, and with the money Momma had made from the sale, she would have more than enough to finish furnishing the new apartment with all brand-new pieces.

The second day was spent at Uncle John's cabin. Momma moved quickly and methodically, tossing out the old clothing, documents, trinkets, and tools. I was far slower and more sentimental. I didn't allow Momma to see my tears as they flowed continuously. Whenever she neared or asked me something, I would quickly wipe away any moving droplets of water from my skin and answer as if I had my full composure. Perhaps she could see through the ruse. I wasn't sure.

We ventured back to our house for a quick lunch. While we were there, Momma received the call from Mr. Barnes that would force her back to the motel. A main pipeline had broken beneath the building, causing a major flood throughout most of the first-floor rooms. Mr. Barnes desperately needed Momma there to help him sift through and control the damage.

"I'll be back first thing in the mornin'," Momma instructed. "Finish clearin' the cabin. Don't bother keepin' anything. Toss it all. It needs to be clear. I only offered the furniture in the house. The new owners are expecting the cabin to be completely empty."

I agreed and watched her peel off into the late afternoon. I returned to the cabin to continue the progress Momma and I had made, when I heard a car pull up. My heart raced as I moved to see who it was: Kenneth.

"Please," he started the moment he saw me near the open doorway, "please just hear me out."

"No!" I screamed, my voice a mixture of fear and anger. "Get out of here, Kenneth! Right now, before I call Sheriff Haviland. You're not welcome here."

Kenneth didn't argue. He just waited until I finished yelling.

"Would ya at least let me say what I need to say?" he begged, cocking his head.

Hoping it would lead to his leaving, I allowed him to speak.

"I know ya don't wanna see me, and I know ya hate me," he began, his voice wavering with nervousness. "I don't blame ya. I know I've let ya down. I know life has been very difficult for ya recently with losin' your uncle and all. Still, I've never stopped lovin' ya, Genevieve. I've never felt this way about anyone. I can't go on with my life without ya. I know you're mad at me now, but will ya please allow me to show ya that the life I can give ya will be the one you've always hoped for."

I stared, hoping he was through.

"Whaddya say?" he finally asked when I failed to say a word.

"How'd ya know I was here?" I asked.

He shook his head, obviously confused by my question. "Well," he fumbled, "I...uh...well, I been followin' ya. I been hangin' out around the old ladies' farm, hopin' to catch ya alone, just to talk. I saw your momma arrive and pick ya up. I stayed way back but followed ya here. I've been waitin' at the foot of the driveway for nearly two days now. I planned to approach when your momma was still here, but I jumped at the chance when I saw her leave. I mean ya no harm, Gen. Only love. Pure love. I promise."

I sighed. "Kenneth," I said, clearing my throat, "I appreciate you goin' so far outta your way to say all this, but I just can't help nor control how I feel. I don't feel the same way about you as you do me. We shared some nice times. It was fun to fanaticize about a future together. I was excited to have your baby, but all that ended. Perhaps it was meant to be. I'm sorry, Kenneth, but I don't love ya. I care for ya. I want the best for ya. But I simply do not want to share my life with ya."

Kenneth stood completely still, almost as if he were trying to avoid the eyesight of some prowling bear or panther. Finally, he began to cry.

"Please, Gen," he sobbed, falling to his knees. "I can't live without ya! I can't!"

He latched onto my ankles. I just stared down at him with pity. What was I going to do?

Thankfully, eventually Kenneth pulled himself together and started to move toward his chocolate-brown Lincoln. Obviously still resistant to defeat, he turned one last time to face me.

"Ya know where to find me, Gen," he stated, his face swollen from heavy crying. "I'll always be here for ya, waitin'. Prayin' you'll come around. We're young, and life is long. Please know that I'll always be waitin' for ya. No matter what happens. I'll always want you."

I nodded but didn't say a word. I watched in a relieved exhalation as he maneuvered the massive car off the property. Within a few minutes, the shiny-new Lincoln was completely out of sight.

***

I AM NOT SURE how Dr. Reynolds knew I was back at home. Perhaps he had followed me as well. Perhaps his son had informed him. Or perhaps he had just taken a lucky chance. But, to my bad luck and misfortune, he arrived unexpectedly

211

later that night. I had already fallen asleep on Momma's old mattress; we had broken down and thrown out the rusted old frame. The sound of his knocking startled me into a fearful awareness. The faint sight of the man I had only known a brief time filled my vision as I slowly cracked open the door. He appeared nervous but was forceful with his words.

"We need to talk," he declared, moving into the house. He brushed past me and walked straight to the kitchen table. It appeared that he knew his way around.

"Um...Doc—um..."

"Please, let's not make this any harder than it needs to be."

His interruption to my stumbling shock allowed me to view what was tucked between his ribcage and right arm: a small leather satchel. He had brought something with him.

"I'm here to compromise with ya," he stated, motioning for me to take a seat with him at the table.

I visibly declined by remaining still at the door. My heart was pounding so loudly inside my chest that I swore I could hear the liquid sizzle of the warm blood as it surged and pulsated through the veins and inner chambers of my entire body. I had to focus on my breathing to avoid collapsing to the floor.

"My son is absolutely in love with you," he continued. "I've never seen him this way. As a doctor, I'm worried about his overall heath. Physical, mental, and otherwise. He's barely eatin', barely sleepin', and I fear he's drinkin' to help him deal with his pain."

I just stared at the doctor, in complete disbelief that he was here, much less of what he was saying.

"I'm here to make ya an offer."

I shook my head, an instant and uncontrolled reaction.

"I'm gonna pay ya to disappear. To leave. To go as far away as your heart desires. I'll pay for everything. The expense of the move, your transportation, even the…" His word trailed alongside the movement of his eyes. "Wait," he sounded confused. "Are ya movin'?"

"Uh…" I didn't know how to respond. I had no idea what to say.

"Did your momma sell all this?"

I nodded. It was enough.

"Where ya goin'?"

"Gatlinburg," I heard my voice blurt. Silently, I mentally kicked myself for saying anything at all.

"Hmm." The doctor rubbed his chin as he appeared to scramble through the racing thoughts in his head. "Not far enough," he finally stated. "I want ya to go to California."

I stared at him, baffled, yet still far too fearful and intimidated to fully produce a complete and proper reply.

"I'll pay ya in cash. In full. No installments. I've already arranged the transportation to Knoxville. You'll fly to California from there. San Diego. Beautiful city. My wife and I honeymooned there."

"I…"

"Come," Dr. Reynolds commanded, standing to his feet and moving toward me. "The sooner, the better. You can phone your momma from the airport."

"No!" I finally heard myself scream. I bolted from the door and into the corner of the kitchen. "I'm goin' with my momma. I ain't movin' by myself to California!"

The doctor glared at me for a long moment before finally smiling. "You're a young, pretty girl," he spoke softly, his voice now light and gentle, not heavy and forceful as it had been since he arrived. "You'll make new friends, fall in love, have a boyfriend. You'll keep a man satisfied."

The last part of his statement sent an instantaneous shiver down my spine.

"What do ya mean?" I asked, some force within me taking control of my voice.

His eyes sparkled in the faint light, but he didn't reply.

"Let's go," he nodded toward the open door. "Knoxville is a good drive from here and the flight leaves at sunrise."

I started to panic. What was I going to do? How was I going to get out of this? There was no other way out of the house besides the front door, which Dr. Reynolds was easily blocking. Also, what was in that brown satchel under his arm? A knife? A gun? How far was he willing to go to get what he wanted?

"I'm not leavin'," I heard myself say. "I'm sorry."

I watched as the doctor closed the front door with a loud and obvious sigh of frustration.

"I was hopin' ya wouldn't make me do this," he stated matter-of-factly as he inched toward me. He moved the leather satchel from under his arm and untied the knot that kept it secured. He pulled out a large stainless-steel syringe, the exact kind I had seen more than once at Uncle John's cabin.

I ran into the bathroom and slammed the door shut. Locking the flimsy doorknob, I turned my body, pressed my feet against the side of the old porcelain tub, and pushed my back against the door with all my might.

The door began to break apart as the doctor kicked and slammed his body against it. It didn't take long for him to damage it enough to grab me by the hair and pull me out of the room.

"Time for a nap, ya little slut," he whispered, attempting to jab the needle into my shoulder. "Maybe I shoulda brought the GHB for old times' sake."

In that moment, I knew it was true: everything Uncle John had accused this man of, was true. I didn't know what GHB was, but my brain instantly connected it to the bottle and rag Uncle John had described in his note. This epiphany provided me the strength to fight back.

"No!" I raged, with every ounce of my being. The unexpected outburst caused Dr. Reynolds to fall flat against his backside. The needle fell to the floor beside him.

"It's true!" I screamed, a mixture of sweat and tears falling into my eyes. "You did rape me!"

The doctor just smiled, the same faint glint I had seen in his stare just a bit earlier reprising its swirl atop his steady gaze.

"There's just somethin' about unconscious teenage pussy," he confessed, moving to lift his body from the floor. "Don't worry, I ain't gonna fuck ya again, especially now that my son has been there. I'm just here to see to it that ya get on that airplane and never come back."

"What about my baby?" I heard myself ask, unsure as to where that thought even came from. "Did you do somethin' to my baby?"

My question seemed to stun him. He stopped his movement, his body only halfway into a full stance. He remained quiet before lowering his head.

"I took care of it the last night you slept at my house," he confirmed in a somber and low tone. "That was my last chance. After you had fallen asleep, I knocked you out real good. Kenneth too. I couldn't risk either one of ya wakin' up during that. I did it cleanly. Carefully. It had to be done."

I felt my knees begin to buckle. The room around me began to spin. I gripped the chair in front of me for support.

"No!" a voice in my head shouted. "You must stay strong! You must stay alert! You must fight your way out of this!"

Dr. Reynolds began to move toward me, the large syringe gleaming in his right hand.

"I'm sorry for the baby," he continued in the same low tone. "That broke my heart. Like it or not, it was my first grandbaby, but I just knew Kenneth wasn't ready to be no daddy. You're both too young. He needs to finish school. He needs to go to college. He needs to be a success. He's my son. Kenneth Reynolds, son of Sevierville's one-and-only doctor. I can't have him runnin' out here livin' the hillbilly life with some mountain girl. What would people think about that?"

He paused, allowing his eyes to move over my entire body.

"I mean, hell, I don't blame him. You are one sweet piece of ass. But still, a girl like you is only worth fuckin', not marryin'."

He darted toward me; I pushed the chair at him. He stumbled. I managed to move to the sink, but he grabbed my arm. I felt the needle pierce my skin.

"No!" I screamed, turning to bite his hand.

"Ah!" the doctor cried out in pain, dropping the syringe. I ducked as he swung at me with a closed fist. I fell to my knees, struggling to crawl away. Immediately, I felt my head grow heavy, my arms wobbling under the weight of my upper body. The drug was working. I was starting to fade.

Then, the familiar ringing behind my ears vibrated around the backside of my skull. In the haze of the room around me, the house filled with a blinding white light. Every feature and facet of the room disappeared into the brightness. I could hear Dr. Reynolds yelling behind me.

"What is that?" he screamed, his voice now high and fearful. "What is that?"

I lifted my head to see the living room window. It was barely visible within the thickness of the white light. There, side by side, were the three figures, the same ones I had seen several weeks prior at the edge of the woods on the backside of Ms. Edna and Janice's farm. Now, though, they were just feet before me. The ringing vibrated stronger. Swallowed by the light, my last memory was that of Dr. Reynolds's panicked howling as the three figures moved toward him. Then, everything went black.

***

WHEN I CAME TO, I was in Ms. Edna and Janice's bed. There was no one around me. The cabin was quiet; the sun was just beginning to seep in through the lace curtains.

I sat up. The door was closed. I was in my nightgown. What happened? How did I get here?

I moved to the door and opened it. I could see Ms. Edna sitting alone at the kitchen table. The room was still surrounded in the barrage of bouquets Kenneth had brought, each one in a different state of decay.

"Ms. Edna," I spoke, my voice dry and hollow.

I startled her. She jumped, turning her head in my direction. She stared for a moment before managing a verbal response.

"Hey, hon." She smiled. "How ya feelin'?"

I shook my head, allowing my eyes to dart around the room.

"How did I get here?" I asked, suddenly panicked. "Where's Dr. Reynolds? I was at the old house. He came there and... there were these things...this light..."

"Shh," Ms. Edna cooed, moving to my side and guiding me into the living room.

She wrapped me in the handsewn quilt from my cot and handed me a mug of freshly brewed ginger tea, her staple comfort splurge.

"You been out a few days, love," she finally revealed once my breathing had calmed and fallen into an even pace. "Your momma is here too. She just ran into town to collect some things."

"Wha—I—"

"Shh," Ms. Edna whispered. "Just listen, babe. I'm gonna tell ya everything."

I listened in a shocked silence as Ms. Edna detailed the events that followed my last memory from inside the house with Dr. Reynolds. According to her, Momma had found me the next morning atop her old mattress. There was no sign of Dr. Reynolds. When Momma couldn't wake me, she brought me here to Ms. Edna, fearful I wouldn't make it through the just more than half-hour journey to the county hospital. Together, Momma and Ms. Edna concluded that I was heavily sedated, but not in any real mortal danger. They decided to keep a round-the-clock watch over me until I was awake. Later that evening, someone phoned from Sevierville. Dr. Reynolds had been found, stripped naked, in front of the county courthouse. He was standing still, his eyes closed, his full nudity on display for the whole world to observe. Only, there was one very important thing missing. Well, important to him, I would suppose: his penis. Below a thickness of dark-brown pubic hair, Dr. Reynolds now resembled a woman. His sexual organ was gone. Cut. Castrated. Further examination had found that he was still able to urinate; a small hole had been left within the smoothness of flesh, connected to his original urethra. The rest of him, though, was gone, surgically cut and removed in a complete and precise procedure. Most of the town had gathered by the time the paramedics arrived to remove him from the scene. He stood on his own, but he was completely unconscious. He only awoke just as the team of paramedics led his naked body through the crowd of onlookers and to the waiting ambulance. They said even Mrs. Reynolds witnessed the entire ordeal. They had to send a second ambulance to transport her after she fainted and fell onto the street curb.

I couldn't help but laugh as Ms. Edna concluded the story. The image of a naked and castrated Dr. Reynolds was not only amusing and hilarious, but a karmic relief. The sudden laughter didn't last long as I began to remember the events of that night: the white light, the three figures.

"I saw the three figures, Ms. Edna," I spoke softly, tugging the quilt around me. "They was at the house. They had this bright white light and—"

"I know, sweetheart." Ms. Edna nodded. "I saw 'em, too."

"What?" I asked, waiting on bated breath for more information.

"They came here again. That night. I had just gotten into bed. Janice was already there asleep. She had been out since about an hour after supper. It was late by the time I finally turned in. I awoke to a commotion and saw the orange glow. Janice was no longer in the bed. I ran out front and saw 'em. The three men. They stood just off to the side of the front pasture, the orange light glowing brightly behind them. I saw Janice walkin' toward 'em. I called out for her. She turned and smiled. I didn't go after her. I don't know, I can't explain it, but I just knew she had to go with 'em. She wanted to. She was never the same after she disappeared that time. Somethin' had changed in her. She was far calmer and more peaceful. It was if she had been waitin' for 'em to come back for her. I just felt this was what was meant to be. I watched her walk until she met them near the tree line. They all moved together into the orange light and were gone. I know that was the last time I will ever see her."

I shook my head, terrified and confused.

"Ms. Edna, no, there has to be—"

"It's what she was waitin' for. It's what she wanted. They had prepared her for this."

"Prepared her for what?" I questioned, annoyed as much as clueless.

"Prepared her to save you."

It all came back to me: the three days missing, the reappearance at the Burnses' farm, the castrated goats. Had Janice done this to Dr. Reynolds? How though? How was that physically possible?

My mind continued to race for impossible answers as Ms. Edna finished the story. The event had made headlines nationwide. People everywhere knew of the castrated doctor found standing still and naked in front of the Sevier County Courthouse. As horrific as it was, most people, especially those outside of the area, found the entire ordeal to be outlandish and laughable. Dr. Reynolds's loss was a newspaper editor's dream.

Momma returned later that afternoon. Ironically, she had just come from the courthouse. The final transfer of the property deeds had been processed there. She was now free of our old homestead, a healthy sum of money now finding a place safe within her bank account.

Despite the overwhelming enormity of all that had recently occurred, we spent the rest of the afternoon talking and giggling like girlhood friends. Momma slept on the couch, while I tossed and turned on my cot. So much now fell into place. So many mysteries now had answers, and questions found their resolution. Yet it opened even more depths of the unknown as I began to ponder it all further. So there really were strange men from the sky watching out for me? They weren't the ones responsible for my night terrors, but Dr. Reynolds and his arsenal of knockout drugs were? I hadn't had a miscarriage, but an unconscious abortion? As much as it all terrified me, I found peace in finally knowing the truth, as out of this world as it was. I thought about Janice, her fear of the visitors and how that had changed after they presumably took her. I agreed with Ms. Edna: Janice wouldn't be back. Wherever she went, she had wanted to go. She never said it, but her calmness and peace upon her return did suggest a shift in her existence. There was an air of patience and waiting. Not to die, but to move beyond. I could tell Ms. Edna was heartbroken, but she also seemed at peace knowing what could never truly be known. I fell asleep that night for the first time in ages with nothing but the sound of my own breathing leading the way. No thoughts, no worries, no mysteries, and no night terrors. Nothing but peace and silence.

***

MOMMA AND I TOOK Ms. Edna into town the next day. It was her first outing in years. She said she hadn't ventured into Sevierville since she retired as principal of Sevierville High School, some two decades or so ago.

The three of us strolled along Main Street, window shopping, laughing, talking, and sharing stories of days gone by. I saw Susan Bellman peering at us as we strolled past Bellman's Dress Shop. In fact, the eyes of every passerby locked on us as we moved down Main Street. Even when we sat at a table inside the café, enjoying some coffee and pastries, the whole dining room gawked and gazed at us the entire time we were there. Just as we were gathering our belongings to leave, Emily Watson entered the café with her mother, Pamela, and two best friends, Tabitha Paul and Beverly Bishop. The entire café fell silent.

Emily glared at me as Momma, Ms. Edna, and I moved toward them. Pamela Watson stepped in front of Momma just as we were about to approach the door.

"You have a lot of nerve showin' your face in town," she snarled, her voice heavy with obvious rage. "What a shame your daughter turned out to be just like ya."

My heart skipped as I sensed Momma tense with anger.

"Please move, Pamela," she said plainly, attempting to hide her true emotion.

Pamela didn't budge. You could feel the energy of the café rise with anticipation.

"You aren't welcome here, Eva," Pamela scowled. "How many times must ya be told that?"

Pamela finally moved aside when Momma pushed forward. Ms. Edna and I followed. I could feel Emily glaring at me as I passed her, but I refused to meet her gaze.

We didn't mention the incident as we returned to Momma's car and ventured back to Ms. Edna's.

Finally, just as we rounded the bend that would return us to the farm, Momma revealed the truth that had eluded me my entire life: the truth of who my father was, the reason Pamela Watson despised Momma, which also explained why her daughter, Emily, despised me.

"When I was seventeen," Momma started, keeping her eyes fixed on the country road before us, "I had an affair with Jeffery Watson, Emily's daddy."

Ms. Edna placed her hand over mine as Momma continued to speak.

"He was already married to Pamela. It was wrong. We both knew it. Still, it happened."

I could feel my heart pounding. It felt like it was lodged in my throat.

"You was the result. It only lasted a few weeks. Jeffery tried to do the right thing by me by payin' for ya. Some kinda monthly child support or somethin', but Pamela refused. Rightfully so, I was outcasted by the townsfolk. Not that I was well-liked to begin with due to our family history and all. Still, maybe I shoulda told ya all this before. I just didn't want to burden ya with it. But you're old enough now to understand, and hopefully, you'll be able to forgive me."

To my surprise, I didn't react emotionally to this revelation. A part of me would have thought I would have been devasted by the news that Emily Watson was my half sister. Perhaps I was in shock, but it didn't bother me; it didn't upset me. In fact, I really didn't care at all.

"You okay, hon?" Ms. Edna asked, smiling at me.

I nodded, smiling back at her and then at Momma, who peered at me nervously through the rearview mirror.

Later that evening, Momma and I sat alone together on Ms. Edna's front porch swing.

"Are ya mad at me?" she asked quietly, nervously shifting her fingers around her thumbs.

"No, Momma," I said softly. "I'm glad ya told me."

"I'm sorry," Momma whispered, her voice breaking with tears. "I was so afraid to tell ya about all this. So afraid it would hurt ya."

I placed my hands over hers.

"It gives me peace, Momma," I confirmed. "Now that I know who my daddy is, I don't have to wonder about it anymore."

"Are ya gonna try to see him?" Momma asked, turning her head to face me.

I thought for a moment before finally shaking my head.

"No, Momma," I said. "I don't think so."

"I mean, you can if ya feel ya need to. Don't let Pamela or Emily stop ya. You have every right to—"

"He may have fathered me, but he was never a daddy to me," I interrupted her. "The man who filled that role is no longer with us. I wish to just remember it all that way. Mr. Watson never tried to do anything for me. Uncle John had his demons, and they caused him to fail me, but it doesn't erase the years he succeeded in lookin' out for me, carin' for me, watchin' out for me when you wasn't around. I don't feel the need to get to know the man who didn't do any of that for me when I needed it most."

Momma smiled and gripped my hands in hers. We held onto each other as we moved the old swing in the dark.

***

I COMPLETED MY HOMESCHOOLING six months later. Principal Lindsay had the school board issue me a diploma. I had done it. I had graduated high school. Mr. Lindsay said I could walk

225

with my class when the time came, but I opted not to. I was eager to start my life in Gatlinburg.

I had spent two weekends a month with Momma in Gatlinburg over the course of the last six months. During that time, I had learned to assist her at the motel. Mr. Barnes was planning to retire within the year, so I was eligible to become assistant manager when Momma formally took over his role as sole lead manager. Momma's temporary assistant manager had long given up on the stressful position some several months back. During this time, I also got to know Derek better. Slowly but surely, I had fallen in love with him, and he with me. On a cold, clear night just before Christmas, Derek proposed. He had saved enough money to buy me a beautiful golden ring with a single, small diamond. It was simple and subtle, but meant the entire world to me. Momma and Ms. Edna were so very proud. I touted the ring around like a queen flashing the royal crown jewels.

Just before I left Locust Ridge for good, Kenneth appeared at Ms. Edna's farm one final time. I agreed to speak with him and asked Ms. Edna to remain inside the cabin while Kenneth and I walked the perimeter of the property. I knew she would be watching as closely as she could to ensure that there were no reprises of Kenneth's previous temper tantrums. There weren't. To my shock, he had come to tell me that he had been accepted to a school in Michigan and would be leaving in a month. Kenneth had graduated high school the previous school year and had spent most of his time dealing with his depression and discontent with the help and assistance of the whisky bottle. He didn't work and simply bummed around his parents' house or one of his friends' couches. Finally, he met a girl, Patty Tanners, a quiet girl I had been semi-acquaintances with back in school, and they planned to marry. She was to move with him to Michigan. I was happy for Kenneth. I could tell he was excited about his future.

He didn't bring up his father, and I didn't dare mention him. I didn't know if Kenneth knew the truth Dr. Reynolds had revealed to me that night at the old house. I certainly never told him and would never tell him, and as far as I knew, his father was alive and well, although he had retired his practice and retreated to staying home most of the time. Various national newspapers and tabloids often tried to interview him. There was still such an interest in the mystery that continued to shroud what had happened to him. Personally, I had stopped thinking about it. That whole night was such a blur, and the prospect that he had been castrated by Janice with the help and guidance of some unseen visitors from presumably outer space was simply far too unbelievable to me, despite what I had witnessed with my own eyes in the house that night. Yes, Janice had disappeared, and the doctor's privates were mutilated yet still functional, but I just could not wrap my brain around the prospect of what was being suggested. Some of the press had picked up on reports of strange lights over the skies of Locust Ridge, a blade-wielding old woman who had turned up naked on a neighboring farm, castrating some of their male goats, and even the presence of strange beings hidden within the trees. Groups of self-proclaimed UFO and paranormal researchers descended upon the town. They interviewed townsfolk who had claimed to see these the strange lights in the night sky, even some mountain folk who had told tales of encountering the mysterious beings themselves. The group even flocked to the supposed landing spot out in the woods just beyond Ms. Edna's property line. To my relief, they knew nothing of me and my connection to the now infamous doctor. They came and went but never bothered Ms. Edna and me, besides leaving a note in the mailbox with a phone number and a request to contact them regarding any sightings or strange occurrences. I discovered the note and Ms. Edna destroyed it. We had no interest in adding to the sudden novelty that had befallen the area.

I hugged Kenneth when he left that night. I knew I'd never see him again. I could tell he knew it too. I wished him luck and told him to write me. I didn't disclose my plan to move to Gatlinburg, and I certainly did not mention my engagement to Derek. When Kenneth had arrived that night, I had taken off my ring and hidden it beneath my pillow. I just didn't want to go there with him. I felt he was there to make peace with me and our past, so I allowed him that. I didn't feel he needed to know anything about my future.

Once I had moved to Gatlinburg, I ventured back to Ms. Edna's every Saturday evening. I would stay the night and return home early Sunday morning. Sometimes, Derek would join me. He would take the cot, while I shared the bed with Ms. Edna.

I could see Ms. Edna growing weaker and feebler. She spoke of Janice often. I could tell she missed her.

The last time I saw Ms. Edna alive was just a regular Sunday morning. Like always, we shared a pot of coffee and munched on fresh fruit, toast, and eggs that were still warm from the hen house. I had been urging Ms. Edna to come and live with us in Gatlinburg. I shared the one-bedroom apartment with Momma, but Momma had arranged for Ms. Edna to reside in one of the motel rooms, free of charge. Ms. Edna refused. She insisted on remaining on the farm until her death. I would make it a point to try to complete the more laborious farm chores when I arrived each Saturday evening, but even still, the day-to-day upkeep of the farm was rugged and grueling, especially on a woman who was nearing her mid-eighties.

I kissed Ms. Edna goodbye later that final Sunday morning, waving at her from the drivers-side mirror of Momma's blue Buick as I journeyed the pathway toward the mountain road that would take me back to Gatlinburg. When I arrived the following Saturday, I found her on the front porch swing, her eyes closed, her head slumped forward, and a mug of cold ginger tea still clasped in her hands. I cried alone as I laid my head on her lap. After an hour or so, I called Momma, and she and Derek arrived to help me arrange for Ms. Edna's burial.

Although we had announced it in the local paper, no one showed up the following weekend when we buried Ms. Edna beneath an old dogwood tree at the back of the property. I thought for sure Principal Lindsay would attend, but he didn't. Even in death, Ms. Edna remained an outcast, the life she had shared with Janice still deemed sinful and abominable in the eyes of the people of Sevierville and nearby Locust Ridge. I cried as the funeral director and his assistants covered the simple oak coffin with the fresh dirt from the hole they had just dug. Above the plot, we placed two wooden crosses. One said Edna, the other, Janice.

∗∗∗

IT WAS JULY 1975 the last time I saw the stars move over Locust Ridge, Tennessee. My daughter, Janice, now just over a year old, cooed in my arms while Momma and I enjoyed the old front porch swing at what had been Ms. Edna and Janice's farm. The cabin and surrounding property remained empty a year and a half after Ms. Edna's death. Momma and I would occasionally sneak up here just to escape the noise and busyness of Gatlinburg. Derek had opened his own motorcycle rental and repair shop and was often too busy to join us. I was happy with Derek. I loved him so deeply. Our daughter was conceived on our honeymoon, which was nothing more than a romantic stay at one of the nearby Gatlinburg hotels. Momma and Mr. Barnes had arranged for us to enjoy the honeymoon suite, which was as gaudy and tacky as one would imagine. But it was in what was considered one of the finest hotels in town, so we were both grateful and appreciative. Our wedding had been a small one. We exchanged vows before the justice of the peace and a small handful of witnesses. I wore a simple white dress, nothing fancy nor over the top, just a sleek number Momma and I had found at one of the local dress shops. Derek wore slacks and a fitted jacket. He looked incredible, every bit as handsome as the gorgeous male movie stars of days gone by.

Saving our money, we were able to afford a small wood-framed house in the foothills of Gatlinburg. Within a year, we had a home and a business, and I was working full time as Momma's assistant manager.

Momma had met a man some months prior to my wedding. His name was Randy; he worked at a nearby trucking company, and he doted upon and adored my momma. I was so happy for her, and she appeared to be living on cloud nine most of the time. He and Derek got along just fine, so our shared family time together was always a welcome pleasure.

This time, though, it was just Momma and me, together with little Janice. Obviously, I had named my daughter after Janice Everly. Although I still did not accept the possibility that Janice had anything to do with what had happened that night at the old house with Dr. Reynolds or what had happened to him in the hours that followed, before he appeared naked and genital-less in front of the county courthouse, I still felt a very strong kindred connection with her. I felt, wherever she was, she was still watching out for me, traveling the heavens in a way only she could understand.

I missed Ms. Edna, desperately so. I would often visit the farm alone, just to sit and chat with her at the backyard grave beneath the old dogwood tree. I never said anything to Momma, but despite my adulthood bonding with my mother, Ms. Edna had provided me a connection and companionship that Momma was unable to during those months of my personal turmoil and tribulation. I would always hold Ms. Edna with the utmost respect in the deepest chambers of my heart.

Venturing from the front porch swing, Momma and I prepared a small dinner meal before retiring to bed. We slept side by side in the old bed I had once shared with Ms. Edna from time to time. We kept baby Janice in a small bassinet near the bedside. My old cot remained in the living room. In fact, everything was exactly as it had always been. No one seemed to venture near the farm. With all the talk of mysterious lights and shadowy visitors amongst the trees, people seemed to steer clear of this area. Locust Ridge and nearby Sevierville were now forever synonymous with the likes of a famous country music superstar and a castrated doctor.

I awoke a few hours later to the ringing behind my ears. It had been well over a year since I had last experienced the unmistakable sensation of its deafening vibration. I drifted from the bedroom to the front porch, and from the front porch into the side yard, which overlooked the barn.

There it was: the orange glow. It was the first time I had seen it since the night Janice had disappeared the first time. My heart began to race; beads of sweat quickly formed over my brow. I started to retreat toward the cabin, when something caught my eye. There, just beyond the view of the chicken coop, was the sight of the old dogwood tree, Ms. Edna's grave beneath it. In the bright glow of the fiery orange light, I could see Janice, clear as day, her back turned to me, her attention focused on the grave. I wanted to call out to her, even to run to her, but I remained still and silent. I continued to watch, the minutes passing like seconds. Finally, she turned her head toward the tree line. I followed her gaze to see the three figures, the same ones I had seen the night she had first vanished, as well as the night in the old house with Dr. Reynolds. I looked back to Janice, who nodded her head at the three beings, gave one last look at Ms. Edna's grave, and began what appeared to be a floating movement in the direction of the tree line. Like Janice, the figures appeared to float in place. My heart began to settle, and the cold sweat faded as I witnessed what could only be described as otherworldly. I saw Janice join the figures in the tree line. The orange glow brightened to a sun-like yellow hue. I squinted my eyes as the radiating light became white and heated. Suddenly, my vision focused and I could see clearly. Janice, appearing more youthful than she ever had in the time I had known her, smiled and nodded at me. She was still among the trees of the property line, but I could clearly make out her face. I smiled and nodded in return. The vibrating ring behind my ears intensified, and in a zapping flash of light, she was gone, as were the three figures that had been standing beside her. Although Janice's face had become clear, the figures had remained featureless and shadowed, their thin, sticklike bodies and bulbous heads nothing more than blurry shapes dotting the background of the enormous light.

Now surrounded by darkness, I stood alone in the front yard of the cabin, watching the golden orbs of light flitting and moving in unison over the starry night sky. In contrast to the first time I ever saw them, when there were seven, eight golden circles now dazzled and zipped across the heavens in an exact and replicated dance. I watched them until they flickered and stopped, pausing in a straight line before zipping northward, never to be seen again.

I crawled into the bed beside Momma, lulled back to sleep by the memory of Janice standing in the tree line, her face smiling and bright, her eyes and nodding head certain and sure. I dreamed of Ms. Edna and Janice that night, the two women who had taken me in as one of their own, caring for, feeding, educating, and saving me. Edna Stevens and Janice Everly: the true stars of Locust Ridge, Tennessee.

www.ingramcontent.com/pod-product-compliance
Lightning Source LLC
Chambersburg PA
CBHW050253110726
47898CB00007B/2397